THE
ALWAYS
WAR

Also by Margaret Peterson Haddix

Claim to Fame
Palace of Mirrors
Uprising
Double Identity
The House on the Gulf
Escape from Memory
Takeoffs and Landings
Turnabout
Just Ella
Leaving Fishers
Don't You Dare Read This, Mrs. Dunphrey

The Missing series
Found
Sent
Sabotaged
Torn

The Shadow Children series
Among the Hidden
Among the Impostors
Among the Betrayed
Among the Barons
Among the Brave
Among the Enemy
Among the Free

The Girl with 500 Middle Names
Because of Anya
Say What?
Dexter the Tough
Running Out of Time

THE ALWAYS WAR

MARGARET PETERSON
HADDIX

SIMON & SCHUSTER BFYR

NEW YORK LONDON TORONTO SYDNEY

SIMON & SCHUSTER BFYR

An imprint of Simon & Schuster Children's Publishing Division
1230 Avenue of the Americas, New York, New York 10020

SIMON & SCHUSTER BFYR is a trademark of Simon & Schuster, Inc.
For information about special discounts for bulk purchases, please contact Simon & Schuster Special Sales at 1-866-506-1949 or business@simonandschuster.com.
The Simon & Schuster Speakers Bureau can bring authors to your live event. For more information or to book an event, contact the Simon & Schuster Speakers Bureau at 1-866-248-3049 or visit our website at www.simonspeakers.com.
Book design by Krista Vossen
The text for this book is set in Palatino LT Std.
Manufactured in the United States of America
4 6 8 10 9 7 5 3
Library of Congress Cataloging-in-Publication Data
Haddix, Margaret Peterson.
The always war / Margaret Peterson Haddix
p. cm.
Summary: In a war-torn future United States, fifteen-year-old Tessa, her childhood friend Gideon, now a traumatized military hero, and Dek, a streetwise orphan, enter enemy territory and discover the shocking truth about a war that began more than seventy-five years earlier.
ISBN 978-1-4169-9526-5 (hardcover)
ISBN 978-1-4424-3604-6 (eBook)
[1. War—Fiction. 2. Heroes—Fiction. 3. Computers—Fiction. 4. Post-traumatic stress disorder—Fiction. 5. Science fiction.] I. Title.
PZ7.H1164Aiw 2011
[Fic]—dc22
2010033344

*For Rich and Mark and Doug, in memory of
certain Iraq War debates*

THE
ALWAYS
WAR

CHAPTER

Gideon Thrall stood offstage, waiting in the wings. The announcer hadn't called his name yet, but people craned their necks and leaned sideways to see him. Whispers of excitement began to float through the crowd: "There he is!" "The hero . . ." "Doesn't he just *look* like a hero?"

Then the PA system boomed out, so loudly that the words seemed to be part of Tessa's brain: "And now, our honoree, the young man we will be forever indebted to for our survival, for our very way of life—Lieutenant-Pilot Gideon Thrall!"

The applause thundered through the crowd. Gideon took his first steps into the spotlight. His golden hair gleamed, every strand perfectly in place. His white uniform, perfectly creased, glowed against the darkness around him. He could have been an angel, a saint—some creature who stood above ordinary humans. Even the fact that he walked humbly, with his head bowed, was perfect. At a moment like this most people would have looked too proud, like they were gloating. But not Gideon. He wasn't going to lord it over anyone that he, Gideon Thrall, had just won his nation's highest honor, something nobody else from Waterford City had ever done.

Standing at the back of the crowd with the other kids from the common school, Tessa felt her heart swell with pride.

"I know him," she whispered.

The applause had just begun to taper off, so Tessa's voice rang out louder than she'd intended. It was actually audible. Down the row Cordina Kurdle fixed Tessa with a hard stare.

"What did you say, flea?" Cordina asked.

Tessa knew better than to repeat her boast. The safe response would be a shrug, a cowed shake of the head, maybe a mumbled, "Nothing. Sorry for bothering you." But sometimes something got into her, some bold recklessness she couldn't explain.

Maybe she wanted to brag more than she wanted to be safe?

"I said, I know him." She cleared her throat. "He was my neighbor. We grew up together."

Cordina snorted.

"Hear that?" she said to the kids clustered around her.

Her sycophants, Tessa thought. *Cronies. Henchmen.*

The words she'd found in old books were fun to think about, but they wouldn't provide much protection if Cordina decided that someone needed to beat up Tessa to teach her a lesson.

"Hear what?" one of the sycophants asked, right on cue.

"Gnat over there thinks she deserves some credit for

living on the same planet as the hero," Cordina mocked.

"We were next-door neighbors," Tessa said. She stopped herself from adding, *We made mud pies together when we were little*, though it was true. Possibly. Tessa didn't remember it herself, but way back when Gideon was first chosen for the military academy, Tessa's mother had started showing around a picture of Tessa, about age two, and Gideon, age five or six, playing together in the mud behind their apartment building.

Gideon had looked like a golden child destined for great things even then, even sitting in mud.

Tessa had looked . . . muddy.

Tessa was saved from any further temptation to brag—or embarrass herself—because the general who'd come from the capital just for this occasion stepped to the podium. He held up a medallion on a chain, and the whole auditorium grew quiet. The general let the medallion swing back and forth, ever so slightly, and the spotlight glinted from it out into the crowd. For a moment Tessa forgot that the city auditorium was squalid and dirty and full of broken chairs and cracked flooring. For a moment she forgot that the people in the crowd had runny noses and blotchy skin and patched clothing. She forgot they could be so mean and low-down. For that one moment everyone shared in the light.

"Courage," the general said in a hushed voice, as if he too were in awe. "We give this medal of honor for courage far above the measure of ordinary citizens. Only eleven people have earned this medal in our nation's history. And now Gideon Thrall, a proud son of Waterford City, will be the twelfth." He turned. "Gideon?"

The general lifted the chain even higher, ready to slip it over Gideon's head. Gideon took a halting step forward, as if he wasn't quite sure what he was supposed to do.

No, Tessa thought. To her surprise she was suddenly furious with Gideon. *Don't hesitate now! Be bold! You're getting an award for courage. Act like it!*

Gideon was staring at the medallion. Even from the back of the auditorium Tessa could see his face twist into an expression that looked nothing like boldness or bravery. How could he be acting so confused? Or . . . scared?

"For your bravery in battle," the general said, holding out the medallion like a beacon. He was trying to guide Gideon into place. Gideon just needed to put his head inside the chain. Then everyone could clap and cheer again, and all the awkwardness would be forgotten.

Gideon made no move toward the chain.

"No," Gideon said, and in the silent auditorium his voice sounded weak and panicky. "I . . . can't."

"Can't?" the general repeated, clearly unable to believe his own ears.

"I don't deserve it," Gideon said, and strangely, his voice was stronger now. "I wasn't brave. I was a coward."

He looked at the general, looked at the medallion—and whirled around and ran from the auditorium.

CHAPTER

It felt like Gideon had stolen all the air from the room. For a moment nobody moved; nobody even breathed. Then Cordina, with her finely tuned sense of cruelty, turned to Tessa.

"So, slug," she said. "If you and the hero are so *close*, why aren't you running after him?"

"Maybe I will," Tessa said.

She backed away from Cordina. Her retort was mostly just to keep Cordina from having the last word. But it felt good to move, to pull away from the crowd, which was beginning to unfreeze from the shock. Whispers were starting to ripple around Tessa: "What?" "Did he say 'coward'?" "How could he—"

Tessa couldn't stand to hear any of it. She raced out the

door. Nobody tried to stop her. Even the class monitors were just staring toward the stage, stunned and aghast.

In the hallway outside there was more cracked tile, and broken windows, peeling paint, crumbling plaster. Repairs, of course, were on hold until the war ended. And it never ended.

Tessa stumbled, righted herself, kept running down the hall. The cracked soles of her shoes flapped against the broken tiles. She didn't expect to find Gideon, but the angry words she wanted to shout at him flocked in her mind.

Don't you know what it's like for the rest of us, those of us who aren't heroes? Don't you know how dreary our lives are? Don't you know this was going to be our one golden moment, our one afternoon of pride? Don't you know you ruined it for everyone? You just gave us something else to be ashamed of—

Then she saw Gideon.

He had his golden head bent over an industrial-size trash can. The hero seemed to be vomiting.

"You're just sick," Tessa said, the surprise and relief giving her the courage to actually speak.

Gideon lifted his head and blinked at her. A clammy sheen of sweat spread across his face and clumped in his curls. Up close he looked so young—just a boy, not a man.

"Someone should tell them—I'll go tell them," Tessa said, suddenly energized. The ceremony could be saved after all. Or—she glanced at his sweaty, wrinkled uniform—rescheduled, anyway. Set for another day. "You're just sick, not cowardly." The relief made her giddy. "Even a hero can get the stomach flu."

Gideon reached out and grabbed her wrist, stopping her.

"No," he said. "No. Didn't you hear what I said in there? I was a coward. I am one. I don't deserve any honors. All I did was kill people."

"We're at war," Tessa said. "That's what war is."

But she wanted to pull her arm back. It was thrilling to think of a hero touching her wrist. A killer, though . . .

It's not the same thing, she told herself. *He's just being modest.*

That was the wrong word, and she knew it. She tried to think of something that would make Gideon—and her—see everything the right way again.

"You had to kill the enemy to save your own people," Tessa said.

Gideon stared at her as if she were speaking a foreign language. Perhaps even the enemy's language.

And then others were streaming out of the auditorium— the officials who'd been standing on the stage. The mayor, the city council members, the military men who'd come from the capital . . .

Gideon was still holding on to Tessa's arm.

"Hide," he said. "You don't want to be seen with me."

He jerked on her arm, propelling her toward a crumbling column. And then he let go.

Tessa didn't know if any of the officials had seen her. She didn't know if it mattered. But she stayed behind the column while the officials surrounded Gideon, while they whisked him away.

Her knees trembled so much she had to sit down on the broken floor.

Nobody would ever give me a medal for bravery, she thought.

Rumors flew after the ceremony.

Gideon had been taken to the finest hospital in the country, to be treated for battle fatigue.

Gideon was almost recovered, almost ready to come back for another ceremony. The only problem was setting a date for the general to return to Waterford City. He had a busy schedule. It was hard fitting everything in.

Or—Gideon had already been given his medallion, in a private ceremony. He was so humble; that was the problem. He certainly wanted to share his honor with the entire community, with the entire country. But he didn't feel that he needed to stand on a stage to do that.

There was going to be an official announcement. Maybe next week. Maybe next month.

Tessa slogged through her everyday life. Home. School. Her after-school job scrubbing floors at the hospital. Twice a day she passed the Thralls' door down the hall in the apartment building, on her way to and from the stairs. Once, early on, she paused before it, her fist raised to knock.

What would I say? she wondered.

Back when Gideon had first been chosen to go to the military academy, years ago, Mrs. Thrall had made it clear that she thought she was better than all her neighbors. She didn't mingle. She was the mother of a boy who had beaten the odds—he was one in a thousand, maybe one in a million. No one ever actually released the statistics about how many children were accepted. They were the best of the best of the best. Why break it down any further than that?

Tessa wasn't best at anything. She wasn't even particularly good at scrubbing floors at the hospital. Robots could do a better job than her. But all the robotics companies were dedicated to building machines for the war. That left people like Tessa to scrub floors.

I'm fifteen years old, Tessa thought. *Will I still be scrubbing those floors when I'm thirty? When I'm forty-five? Sixty?*

She didn't knock at the Thralls' door.

And then one day there was an ambulance out front when Tessa got home. She hurried up the stairs, a bad feeling in the pit of her stomach.

It could be here for anyone, Tessa thought. *Mrs. Evers on the third floor has a bad heart. Mr. Singleton never really recovered from that stroke last year. Maybe he died. Even my own parents look so frail sometimes, so beaten down. . . .*

But somehow she couldn't talk herself into worrying about anyone but Gideon.

She reached the fifth-floor landing, her floor. She peeked out. The Thralls' door was open just a crack.

Tessa didn't intend to stop outside it, listening. Or, rather, she didn't intend to get *caught* outside it, listening. But she tiptoed past as slowly as she could.

"—have to keep him medicated," a man was saying, just on the other side of the door.

"He doesn't like the medication," a woman's querulous voice complained. Tessa knew this was Mrs. Thrall. "He says it makes it hard to think."

"Some people are better off not thinking," the man replied.

And then the door began to creak open, and Tessa scurried past it. She yanked her key out, rushing to get into her own apartment before anyone saw her.

Why did it matter?

Tessa didn't know. But as soon as she got the door open and rushed inside, she shoved it shut and stood there breathing hard, her back against the hard wood.

That night Tessa lay in bed, staring blankly up at the ceiling. Her room was small; her bed was narrow. Years ago she'd gotten into the habit of pressing her head against the wall and sprawling diagonally across the mattress, so she could trick herself into believing she had more space than she really did. But now something kept hitting against the other side of the wall.

Tap-tap-tap-thump-thump-thump-tap-tap-tap.

And again.

Tap-tap-tap-thump-thump-thump-tap-tap-tap.

And again.

Tessa remembered whose apartment lay on the other side of the wall.

Tap-tap-tap-thump-thump-thump-tap-tap-tap.

It's just some machine, Tessa told herself. *Maybe Gideon Thrall's honor came with some practical benefit. A washer. A dryer. An automatic vacuum.*

But the tapping and thumping was not quite precise enough to be mechanical. Tessa could hear the very human hesitation between the taps and thumps.

He's listening to music, Tessa told herself. *Tapping his foot. Maybe it's not even Gideon. Maybe it's his mother.*

Tessa couldn't fit the rhythm of the tapping and thumping into any song she'd ever heard. Maybe it was some other kind of rhythm, some kind of code.

Tessa got up and turned on the light. She reached to fire up the ancient laptop computer that sat on her desk, then stopped herself. The kids at school said anything you searched for online left tracks. It could always be traced back to you.

Tessa reached instead for the even more ancient encyclopedia set that had come from her grandparents' apartment when they died. Tessa's mother had wanted to throw the books away, but Tessa had rescued them. Some of the volumes were missing, but fortunately the C and M and S books were in the stack.

Code.

Morse code.

SOS.

Tessa found descriptions of dots and dashes, tapped out in sets of three. Dots and dashes—taps and thumps. It had to be the same.

Gideon Thrall, the biggest hero in the country, was begging for help.

How to get past Mrs. Thrall?

That was Tessa's dilemma. She imagined herself picking locks or climbing ropes strung between her window and the window next door. But every scenario she could dream up seemed like it would end the same way: in a confrontation with Mrs. Thrall, rather than Gideon's rescue.

Tessa lay awake far into the night trying to come up with a workable plan. Long after the thumping and tapping stopped, it occurred to her that she could have studied the Morse code symbols a little longer and come up with a coded reply: *What do you need?* maybe, or, *How can I help?* She tapped the wall once, experimentally, but there was no response. She got out the *M* encyclopedia again and stared at the Morse code key.

She thought about writing out a message she could tap and thump in the morning, but each letter was so complicated. Even if she managed to make Gideon understand her, what would she do if he started desperately tapping and thumping out a lengthy answer? She'd never be able to follow it—and he'd probably be caught.

No, there had to be some other way. . . .

She fell asleep. And though she wasn't aware of any dreams, she woke up in the morning thinking about flowers.

He's a hero. Surely Mrs. Thrall wouldn't be surprised to see some delivery person bringing flowers from an admirer—surely he's gotten lots of flowers before.

It was worth a try.

Tessa herself couldn't afford to buy any flowers—they were a luxury, rarely grown because they were a distraction from the war effort. But she'd seen goldenrod and milkweed growing in the dirt piles behind the apartment, the same spot where she and Gideon had (maybe) once made mud pies. If Tessa picked some of the weeds and wrapped them in paper so only a leaf or two showed—well, wasn't there at least a chance that it would fool Mrs. Thrall?

Tessa crept out into the chilly morning air. It was a Saturday, but weekend workers streamed down the sidewalk, headed for their jobs. All the faces she saw were gray and worn and weary, as if the people had long ago given up any hope of a better life.

Oh, please, Gideon, Tessa thought. *That's why we needed a hero.*

She darted around the building, stepping from one clump of ugly, spiky grass to another. Dew clung to a spiderweb binding several of the taller weeds together, and Tessa wished she could carry that up to Gideon too.

It's so beautiful—wouldn't he see the beauty in it? Tessa wondered.

The kids at school never saw things the same way as Tessa; why did she think that Gideon might? And, anyhow, she wasn't supposed to be finding anything beautiful. She just needed to trick Mrs. Thrall.

Tessa hacked at the plants before her. When she had a big enough bundle to make a convincing bouquet, she went back upstairs to her apartment and wrapped the whole thing in paper. And then, before she lost her nerve, she knocked at the Thralls' door.

"Florist delivery!" Tessa called out.

The door creaked open.

Mrs. Thrall stood before her in a deep purple robe, and for a moment Tessa lost herself staring. The robe was *new*. Where could you buy new things anymore?

"Yes?" Mrs. Thrall said.

Tessa forced herself to stop staring at the robe. She lifted her gaze to Mrs. Thrall's face.

"These are, uh, flowers to be delivered to Lieutenant-Pilot Gideon Thrall," Tessa said. She started to hold them out to Mrs. Thrall, then caught herself. She clutched the bundle of weeds tighter to her chest. "I have orders to deliver them directly into his hands," she added.

Mrs. Thrall frowned. The lines around her eyes were etched much deeper than Tessa would have expected. But Tessa had only ever seen her from afar. It wasn't surprising that Mrs. Thrall looked different close up.

"Your 'orders' are to see him face to face, then," Mrs. Thrall said in a mocking voice.

Tessa's heart sank.

She sees right through me, Tessa thought. *She knows I'm lying.*

But Mrs. Thrall didn't slam the door in her face. For a moment she just stood there silently, watching Tessa. Tessa was sure Mrs. Thrall was noticing Tessa's ratty sweater, her threadbare jeans, the way her dark hair curled in all the wrong directions. Tessa remembered how, even before Gideon went off to the academy—How old was he then? Eight? Ten?—Mrs. Thrall always looked so disapprovingly at girls around the neighborhood who so much as glanced at Gideon. She had a narrowed-eyes glare that all but spoke: *Oh, no. You're not good enough for my son.*

She did this even to pretty girls, girls whose families had money—or, at least, as much money as anyone had in Waterford City.

Tessa wasn't all that pretty, and her family had less money than just about everyone they knew. And yet suddenly Mrs. Thrall took a step back.

"Come in," she said.

"I can?" Tessa asked incredulously. "I mean—thank you."

She stepped into the Thralls' apartment, and Mrs. Thrall closed the door behind her. Immediately something changed in Mrs. Thrall's expression, as if she'd put on a mask.

Or taken one off.

"Gideon's room is over there," Mrs. Thrall said, pointing. Her face sagged, as if keeping up appearances was beyond her now. She didn't look like the haughty mother of the hero anymore. She just looked old—old and weary and despairing.

Tessa realized she'd been thinking about everything wrong. Mrs. Thrall wasn't the enemy. She wasn't the obstacle Tessa needed to worry about.

But what *was* Gideon's problem?

"Um, is he . . . ," Tessa began.

"Just go in there!" Mrs. Thrall commanded. "You can see for yourself!"

Mrs. Thrall turned her head away, but not before Tessa saw tears sparkling in the woman's eyes. There was a remnant of her old glare in her expression—*You're not good enough; no one's worthy of my Gideon.* In a flash Tessa understood something she didn't want to understand, something ugly. Mrs. Thrall did think Tessa was one of those girls who threw themselves at boys. She hated Tessa. But she was willing to let Tessa in to see Gideon anyhow, because, because . . .

Tessa's understanding faltered.

"I'm not like that," she said, defending herself.

The disgust in Mrs. Thrall's expression took over.

"You brought him flowers, didn't you?" she sneered. She might as well have said, *You brought him weeds. You're a weed yourself. Trash.*

Tessa stood up straight. She wanted so badly to say, *He asked me to come. He asked for me.*

But it wasn't quite true. Gideon couldn't have known that Tessa lay on the other side of his wall last night. He didn't even know her. Even if they had played together as little kids—even if that mud-pie picture of them together were real, not something Tessa's mother had faked—then Gideon probably didn't remember it any better than Tessa did.

He certainly hadn't recognized Tessa back at the auditorium.

But he was trying to signal someone *last night,* Tessa thought. *Who? Why?*

She looked at the door into Gideon's room, which was closed tight. The door was dark and scarred, as if someone had attacked it with a knife. Lots of doors in the apartment building looked like that, but the scars made Tessa hesitate. She remembered the flat, expressionless tone in Gideon's voice when he'd told her, *All I did was kill people.* She shivered.

"He wouldn't . . . ," she began. Was she going to say, "hurt me"? *"Kill me"*? About Gideon Thrall? The biggest hero in Waterford City history?

Mrs. Thrall recoiled.

"He doesn't even get out of bed," she snarled.

Mrs. Thrall reached past Tessa to twist the doorknob and push the door open. And then she shoved Tessa forward and shut the door behind her.

Trapping Tessa in Gideon's room.

CHAPTER

The room was dark.

In the time it took Tessa's eyes to adjust, she had to fight down panic: *What could be wrong with Gideon? What's wrong with Mrs. Thrall? Why do I feel like I'm being . . . sacrificed?*

And then Tessa could see ordinary objects around her: a desk. A chair. A bed. Gideon's form lay sprawled across the bed as if he'd fallen there—fallen from some great height, maybe, in a way that left him too broken to get back up.

Tessa remembered that she'd come there hoping to help.

"Um, hello?" she said, in a near whisper. "Your mother said it was okay for me to come in. And, uh . . ."

She let her voice trail off, because it didn't seem that Gideon could hear her. Maybe he was asleep.

Maybe he was dead.

Why hadn't she figured out a way to answer his call for help sooner?

Gideon turned over.

"You saw my mother," he murmured, the words little more than breaths. "Did you see the blood on her robe?"

Blood? Tessa thought.

"N-no," she said, stuttering in her confusion. "Is she hurt? Or—are you?"

She wasn't sure if she should turn around to go help Mrs. Thrall or step closer to Gideon to help him—or just flat out run, to save herself. But Gideon was opening his mouth to talk again, and she had to know what he was going to say.

"They gave her that robe," Gideon said. "Because of me. Because of what I did. It's made of blood. Blood and bones and death . . ."

His voice trailed off. He was staring up at the ceiling—the blank, bland, ordinary ceiling—but his face contorted as if he were watching some unspeakable horror.

"I brought you flowers," Tessa said, and it was ridiculous; this wasn't what you said to someone who looked as anguished as Gideon. But she felt like she had to get him to look away from that ceiling, to stop him from screaming or wailing or whatever he was about to do. (Murdering someone? *No, no, don't think that,* she commanded herself.)

Tessa looked down at the bundled greenery in her arms. The weeds were already wilting.

"Or, actually, they're not exactly flowers," Tessa said, because she couldn't stop herself from talking. "Not what most people would call flowers. That was just my excuse to get in. I heard your SOS last night. Your Morse code. Your—is there something I can do to help?"

Now, that did seem to be the right thing to say. But at first it didn't make any difference. Then Gideon began turning his head, an excruciatingly slow motion. And even when he was gazing toward Tessa, he couldn't seem to focus his eyes on her, standing right there, rather than whatever he thought he saw beyond her.

"You're the girl from the auditorium," he finally said, blinking.

In spite of everything Tessa felt a tingle of pleasure: *He remembers me! The handsome, heroic, amazing Gideon Thrall remembers me!*

"Yes. I live next door," she said, pointing to the wall behind him. Somehow it seemed like she was trying to brag again. Like she was her mother, showing around a picture that was probably faked. Trying for some reflected glory she didn't deserve. "That's how I heard you last night."

Gideon lifted his head from his pillow. He squinted. He was trying so hard to see her.

Tessa felt honored.

"I need a computer," Gideon said. His head fell back against the pillow, as if the exertion of looking at Tessa had been too much for him. "They won't let me have a computer."

"I have a computer," Tessa offered. "I can run and get it—"

"No!" Gideon thundered. He hit his fist against the wall, and for a moment Tessa feared that he was trying to break it down. He could punch a hole in it and reach into Tessa's room and take whatever he wanted that belonged to her. Would she let him? Would she have to? Was that what she'd set in motion, coming here?

All this flashed through Tessa's mind even as Gideon's fist opened and his hand slid helplessly down the wall.

"They'd see you," Gideon whispered. He was staring at the ceiling again. "They watch."

"Who?" Tessa asked.

"You know," Gideon whispered.

Tessa didn't think she did. Clearly, he didn't mean Mrs. Thrall. And as far as Tessa knew, there wasn't a Mr. Thrall, or he'd died or vanished before Gideon was born.

Then she remembered how everybody had watched Gideon as he stood up on the stage. People always watched someone like Gideon.

Someone like Tessa—not so much.

"I'll hide the computer," Tessa told Gideon, trying to placate him. "Nobody will see me bringing it over here. And— I'll tell your mother I'm just getting a vase."

Gideon looked at her again, studying her face, blinking back whatever specters had hidden her from him before.

"Yes," he said.

Tessa felt like she'd just passed some test. She'd pleased him. He liked her. He approved. This made her feel so buoyant that she pushed open the door with great confidence.

Mrs. Thrall was sitting on the opposite side of the living room, as far away as possible. Her face had been taken over with sour disapproval.

"I need a vase for the flowers," Tessa said with great dignity. "I'll be right back."

She left the door of the Thralls' apartment cracked slightly, so she wouldn't have to rely on Mrs. Thrall to let her back in. She rushed into her own apartment, into her own room, feeling glad that her parents weren't anywhere in sight. They were probably still sleeping off the disappointments of last night, of every night of their lives.

They might not awaken all day.

Not me, Tessa thought. *I won't be like them.*

She tucked her small flip-up computer under the front of her shirt and grabbed the first jar she could find from the kitchen.

Back in the hallway she got prickles at the back of her neck. Somehow she did feel like she was being watched now, like someone was paying very close attention to what she was doing.

The hallway was empty.

I'm a girl taking a vase for flowers to a friend, she told herself. *Who would care about that?*

She kept her arms crossed against her stomach, holding the computer in place. But surely, if anyone was watching, it would just look like she was cold.

She nudged open the door back into the Thralls' apartment. Mrs. Thrall's expression, if anything, had grown even more disapproving while Tessa was away. Tessa just brushed past her and went into Gideon's room.

He was sitting up.

Sitting up!

Quickly Tessa pulled the door shut.

"Do you have it?" Gideon asked.

So that's how his voice sounds with some hope in it, Tessa thought. He seemed like a new person, as radiant in the dim room as he'd looked all those weeks ago onstage, in the spotlight. It was amazing how hope could transform even messed-up hair and an unshaven face and unwashed, rumpled clothes into something as stunning as a hero in a crisp uniform.

"Here," Tessa said, pulling the computer from beneath her shirt. She caught her breath. She'd been holding the computer against her bare skin, and now he was touching the computer, and surely he could feel how her skin had warmed the cold metal. . . .

Gideon flipped the computer over and tore off the bottom panel. He began yanking out wires.

"Hey!" Tessa protested. "Stop that! You didn't say you were going to break it!"

She put her hand over his, trying to pull it back.

"I'm not breaking anything," Gideon said. "I'm masking it. So no one can trace my keystrokes."

Tessa stopped pulling on his hand.

"So it's true, what people say?" she asked. "That everything can be traced?"

"Not everything," Gideon said. "Not if you know what you're doing."

He began putting some of the wires back in, twisting them in different ways. He pulled out a set of tweezers from beneath the mattress and did surgery on some of the circuit cards.

Tessa let her hand slip off his and just watched. After a few minutes he put the bottom of the computer back together and flipped it over and turned it on. He began typing in commands

Tessa had never seen before, bringing up strings of mysterious code. They scrolled across the screen too fast for Tessa to read any of it. But Gideon kept typing, almost endlessly, his coding appearing just as rapidly and indecipherably as the computer's. Did he keep all those incomprehensible strings of letters and numbers in his head? Why? What was he looking for?

Tessa thought maybe he'd forgotten she was there. Then suddenly he stopped. He stared at the screen.

"You won't want to see this," he said. His voice had gone flat again.

"It's my computer," Tessa said stubbornly.

Gideon looked at her. His eyes were so, so sad. Tessa had been around unhappy people all her life, but she'd never seen anything like this. You could drown in that kind of sorrow. You could fall into that grief and never be seen again.

"Don't say I didn't warn you," Gideon said.

He hit a single key, and the long strings of coding vanished. A few numbers still flashed across the bottom of the screen, but Tessa ignored them. Instead, suddenly, she was watching video.

People dressed in odd, colorful clothes were crowded into some sort of marketplace. They swirled randomly from one stall to another, examining piles of melons, heaps of strawberries, oranges that seemed to glow in the sunlight. Children laughed and licked ice cream cones. Mothers snuggled babies tight against their chests and kissed their foreheads and tickled their tummies.

Tessa leaned closer, drawn in. Enchanted.

And then suddenly everyone in the video was looking up and screaming and running. The pillars of the fruit stands fell over, watermelons splattering to the ground, oranges rolling underfoot, people tripping and falling and screaming and screaming and screaming.

Tessa felt the explosion that followed, rather than hearing it. She realized that Gideon must have turned the sound off. But she still felt shaken to her bones. She cringed, as if she expected the ceiling to fall on her own head, the world to come crumbling down around her own body.

On the screen, dust rose up to meet everything that was falling down, falling apart, dying. The dust covered dead babies, dead children, dead mothers. Mercifully, the dust hid everything.

The screen went black.

Tessa couldn't move.

"That's what I did," Gideon said, and his voice was every bit as dead as the babies, the children, the mothers. "That's what everyone's worshiping me for."

He looked toward Tessa, and his eyes were dead now too.

"I killed one thousand six hundred and thirty-two people," he said. "Do you still think I'm a hero?"

Tessa backed away from him, pinning herself against the wall.

"Didn't you have to?" she asked in a small voice. "Wasn't it . . . necessary?"

"Was it?" Gideon asked, and in those two words she saw how completely lost he was. He was trying to find something to stand on, something to hold himself up.

But there was nothing.

"The enemy," Tessa said numbly. "They want to kill us. Starve us. Choke us. To death." She was only mouthing words she'd heard all her life. They didn't seem to have any meaning anymore. Not with all that death seared onto her eyes. "You were killing to protect the rest of us."

"Those babies were going to kill us?" Gideon asked. "Babies?"

"When . . . they grew up . . . ," Tessa whispered.

"They're not going to grow up!" Gideon screamed at her. "I killed them!" He snapped the computer shut and thrust it into her hands. "Go on! Get out of here! Before you're contaminated too. . . . What I did—it was wrong! Evil! Evil! Evil!"

Tessa yanked the door open and ran from him.

In the outer room Mrs. Thrall was sobbing, her face twisted and anguished and destroyed, like Gideon's had been twisted and anguished and destroyed. And now Tessa's was twisted and anguished and destroyed too.

At least Tessa could run away.

Mrs. Thrall wasn't looking at Tessa, but Tessa still paused at the door out into the hallway. Something made her stop and cram the computer back under her shirt, some fear that Gideon was right and somebody could be watching and just the sight of Tessa carrying a computer out of the Thralls' apartment could be dangerous.

How could she care about something like that when all those people were dead?

Tessa ran into her own apartment and into her own room and threw herself across her bed. The edges of her computer, tucked under her shirt, poked into her skin. She shoved it down to the end of the bed. Somehow that wasn't enough. She lifted the edges of the computer—retching just because she was touching it—and all but threw it under her bed. After a moment she dropped her pillow down after it, and then a blanket, too, stuffing both of them on top of the computer as if she could suffocate it.

She still felt as though the images could float up from the computer into her head, like poison.

Or ghosts.

What if the images of all those dying people were still on her computer the next time she turned it on? What if they were always there? What if they were always in Tessa's head?

Those people are always going to be dead. Whether I remember them or not.

"Gideon, you were supposed to be better than the rest of us," Tessa whimpered. "Someone worth admiring."

Tessa heard a door open and a door close. She listened hard, something like hope springing back to life in her heart.

Then she heard a toilet flushing, a door opening, and a door closing again. It had only been one of her parents, stumbling out of bed to use the toilet and then stumbling back to their grimy mattress.

She remembered what she'd thought only a little while ago: *Not me. I'm not going to be like them.*

And yet here she was, wallowing in her despair the same way they always wallowed in theirs.

"No!" she wailed.

She stood up, woozily. She yanked the mattress down from the frame and wedged it against the side of the bed, providing another layer between herself and the computer that had held those awful images. Then she whirled around and ran out of the room, out of the apartment, out of the building.

If she ran fast enough, maybe she could trick herself into believing she had somewhere to go.

After a while her legs cramped, and her lungs rebelled

against drawing in another gulp of air when every breath felt like a blade against her ribs. She slowed to a walk.

She'd been running blindly, darting around corners without any mind to direction, and now she was in a completely unfamiliar part of the city. She wended her way through the blank-faced crowds, people grimly standing in lines, people walking with their heads down, their eyes averted.

She was in a marketplace. But in contrast to the cheerful, sun-dappled place in Gideon's video before the bombs began to fall, this marketplace was full of filth and rot and misery. Toothless old men tried to sell shriveled-up apples rattling around in nearly empty boxes. Glassy-eyed children coughed up phlegm and spat it on the ground. And if some of the phlegm sprayed up onto the apples, nobody bothered wiping it away.

No! Tessa wanted to scream. *Somewhere there's beauty, there's hope, there's love; somewhere it doesn't get destroyed. . . .*

She remembered the delicate, dew-covered spiderweb she'd seen that morning. She knew the dew would be long gone by now, but the spiderweb itself had been like a work of art.

Suddenly she felt like she would die if she didn't look at that spiderweb again.

She began running once more, navigating her way through the crowds, squinting at street signs and turning and asking for directions and asking again when people didn't know. First she got more lost, and then she figured out where she was, and then she got lost again. This happened over and over. The images in her head kept slipping down over her vision—the dying children, the dead babies—and awful thoughts kept pushing their way into her mind. *I thought that he would like me. I wanted him to like me. I still want him to like me. Does that make me evil too?* But she could push back the images, the thoughts. She had a goal now.

Just think about the spiderweb. Remember? And then after you see it, you'll be able to think of other beautiful things, other hopeful things, other things to love. . . .

She hadn't realized how far she'd traveled. It was almost dark when she got back to her own street, approached her own apartment building. She hadn't eaten all day. But she brushed past the front door and hurried around back to the dirt pile where she'd found the weeds and the spiderweb.

Children were playing on the dirt pile now—not toddlers making mud pies, but older boys, fighting.

"This is our hill, and you can't have it!" one yelled as he stood at the top. He was maybe seven or eight, a miniature brute.

"Oh, yeah?" another yelled back. "Who's going to stop me?"

He charged up the hill, his fists out.

Tessa squinted into the twilight, gazing at a spot between the two boys. There, amazingly, the spiderweb still hung between two stalks of foxtail grass, its delicate architecture testifying that everything Tessa wanted to believe in was possible.

And then the two boys crashed into it, flattening it as they rolled down the hill fighting.

"No!" Tessa wailed. She raced up the hill after them. She grabbed them by their shirts and pulled them apart. She was so much bigger and stronger than them that this was easy to do.

"No!" she screamed at them. "Don't you see what you did?" She dropped the two boys and began feeling around on the ground. She wanted evidence. She wanted them to see the ruin they'd made. She wanted them to hurt like she did.

But of course there wasn't even a wisp of the spiderweb left. And of course it had never been anything but another illusion. It had been so beautiful—and yet the spider had built it solely to trap and kill.

Like Gideon looks so handsome, so perfect, so heroic, but all he did was kill. . . .

The two boys looked up at Tessa. They were little, only five or six or seven or eight. But their eyes held no innocence. They were already filled with hate and anger, greed and fear.

Tessa began hitting them.

"Stop it!" she screamed at them, pounding her fists against their backs, their shoulders, their arms. "You're already ruined! You already ruin things!"

The boys fought back, their fists small but well aimed.

"Help us!" they called to the other boys standing around. "Attack!"

And then there was a whole pack beating up Tessa. She scrambled away, leaving behind a hank of her hair in somebody's hand. She could escape from children. But she couldn't escape the new images crowding her mind: the beautiful spiderweb falling, beauty itself revealed as a fake, Tessa's own fists beating up little children. . . .

She ran until she found herself back in her own room, on

the bare bed frame, sobbing into the wall. She started to move away, then changed her mind. She wanted Gideon to hear her crying. She wanted him to know the pain he'd caused, the misery.

But he'd killed one thousand, six hundred and thirty-two people.

Why would he care about one meaningless girl's broken heart?

CHAPTER

Sunday was dark, rainy, and hopeless. Tessa did her best to sleep through as much of it as she could.

Oh, Mom, Dad, is this how you've always felt? Ever since you gave up? She wondered if she'd been too hard on them all along. *What made you give up in the first place? Did you ever see what I saw, people dying in the war? Did you ever know anyone like Gideon?*

She didn't bother standing up, walking into her parents' room, asking the questions out loud.

Even if her parents answered her, how would that make any difference?

Monday morning Tessa had to go off to school. She banged around in her room getting ready, slamming drawers and doors and making as much noise as she could.

Why should Gideon get to sleep late and relax all day? she thought bitterly. *He's not a hero. He's a killer. He said so himself. I saw what he did. He should be in prison.*

There was an uncomfortable echo to that thought: *And what about me? What do I deserve for beating up children? What if I'm every bit as evil as he is, and always have been—I just never got a chance to drop any bombs?*

At school, kids stabbed pencils in other kids' backs and tripped people and started fights in the school cafeteria. It was a school day like any other, but somehow even the pettiest cruelty felt unbearable to Tessa. Cordina Kurdle snapped a rubber band at Tessa's arm, and it was all Tessa could do to keep from bursting into tears. Cordina's henchmen, seeing this weakness, went for an all-out assault of pinches and shoves and jabs every time the teacher looked away.

Tessa finally let the tears out after school, as she hunched over, scrubbing floors at the hospital. Sometimes in the past she'd found ways to make her job almost enjoyable—competing to scrub an entire room as fast as she could, or creating designs on the floor in water and suds. But today it was all she could do just to slide her cleaning rag back and forth across the dingy concrete. Tear-blinded, she reached for her bucket. Her hand struck too low and knocked the whole thing over. The gray, slimy water spilled across the floor she'd just cleaned.

"Clean it up!" the supervisor commanded. "Scrub everything all over again! And I'm docking your pay!"

Either the supervisor didn't notice that Tessa was crying, or—more likely—he didn't care.

Not fair, Tessa thought, after everyone else was gone and it was just her and her bucket and rag in the huge, empty room, all that filthy concrete left to be scrubbed. *This is Gideon's fault. He killed all those people and he's the reason I'm crying and he still gets to have some hope. . . .*

Tessa almost dropped her rag. She froze. Was that right? Could she fling the accusation "still has hope" at someone who'd looked as anguished as Gideon had, just about every single moment she'd spent in his presence?

If he didn't have any hope, what did he want my computer for on Saturday? she asked herself. *Why did he want to look at that video? Was he just hoping to destroy me, too? Or . . .*

She remembered that he'd told her she wouldn't want to see the video. He'd warned her not to look.

So why . . . ?

She remembered how final everything had looked on the computer screen, all those dead bodies, all those lives ended. But evidently it wasn't finished. There was still something Gideon had wanted to see, some reason he had needed to scan those horrific images again.

Was there still something he thought he could change?

Tessa threw down her rag. She left her bucket of water in the middle of the floor and took off running. On alternating steps she thought, *I can stop him,* and *I can help him,* and she didn't know which one she believed.

But what if there really was something she could do?

Then I could be a hero, she thought, running harder. *A real one. Whether anybody else ever knows it or not.*

CHAPTER

Tessa crashed into her room without a fully formed plan in her head. She couldn't decide if it would be best to crank up her computer and scour every archive she could find—study it all intensely—or if it would make more sense to grab the computer and stalk over to the Thralls and confront Gideon, first thing. She was leaning toward the confrontation, just because it would be faster.

But what if he lies? What if he just makes up some story, and I don't know enough to be able to tell if it's true or false?

In the midst of scooping up her computer, Tessa paused just long enough to take a deep breath.

And then she stopped completely.

Her room smelled like paint.

Fresh paint.

Her room hadn't been painted in years.

Tessa whirled around, gazing open-jawed at walls she normally didn't notice.

There. Just above the bed, in the middle of the wall she now knew lay between her bedroom and Gideon's, the paint caught the light and glistened, as if some of it wasn't quite dry.

And—Tessa studied it more closely—in one wide circle that contained the glistening spots, even the dry paint was a slightly different shade of industrial gray than the rest of the walls.

Why—? Tessa wondered. *How*—?

She remembered that a storeroom lay directly below her room. The janitor who occasionally bothered to clean the hallways kept brooms and trash cans in there. It was possible that he had cans of paint there as well.

Instinctively, Tessa looked down. The battered rag rug that she kept across the floorboards was bunched up, slightly out of place.

Tessa kicked it aside.

There, in a spot that had been hidden by the rug before, someone had taken out the nails from a roughly circular area of the floorboards.

Someone? Tessa thought. *Oh, no. I know who did this.*

She looked from the circle of fresh paint on the wall to the circle of unattached boards on the floor. She was working on a theory.

So Gideon wanted to get out of his room without being seen. He cut a hole in my wall, and then pried open a hole in my floor. He crawled through and then tried to erase all signs that he'd been here.

But he couldn't put the nails back in the floorboards to completely cover his tracks because . . . Tessa looked down again. She knew why. *Because he still hasn't come back.*

Was he going to? Or was he gone for good?

Tessa hugged her arms against her chest, as if she were capable of comforting herself. She'd forgotten she was still holding the computer, and the cold metal sent a jolt through her system. She jerked her arms back, tilting the computer crazily.

A thin sheet of paper fell from in between the keyboard and the folded-down screen.

Tessa immediately crouched to pick it up and read it:

I scrubbed this clean. (The computer.)

Forget about me.

Destroy this note, too, of course, and then there will be nothing to link you to any of this.

I'm sorry.

CHAPTER

Tessa crumpled the note in her hand. Then she changed her mind—that was too much like obeying. She smoothed the paper out again on her desk.

. . . then there will be nothing to link you to any of this. . . .

That's it? she thought. *That's the end?*

She had been so pumped for confrontation—and for seeing Gideon again. It was hard to switch gears, to think of having an ordinary evening instead. Just another ordinary evening in a completely ordinary life. Ordinary, dull, tasteless, colorless, pointless . . .

What did you expect? she asked herself angrily. Gideon had told her that very first day to stay away from him.

Because he was protecting me, she thought. *Like he was protecting me telling me not to watch the video of the war.*

But wasn't she linked to him and the war, no matter what? Because wasn't the whole point of the war to protect people like her?

Tessa looked up from the note, because she couldn't stand to keep staring at the brusque words, which might as well have said, *You are nothing to me. You are nothing.* Had he spent ten seconds scrawling out this note? Twenty? Was she worth that little? Couldn't he have even signed his name?

Tessa stared out the window. The streetlights were out again. This happened a lot—with the war on, there wasn't even enough money for spare lightbulbs. And some people said the sudden blackouts were a test, a trial run of what the city would do if the enemy's bombers made it this far past the border.

"Why would anyone bother destroying Waterford City? How could it look any worse with bombs dropped on it than it does now?" was one of the jokes that people told.

Even without streetlights Tessa could make out shapes moving in the shadowed darkness down on the sidewalk. With infrared cameras and night-vision instruments, the enemy would have no trouble picking out people to kill. They could be in some airplane high overhead and then—

Stop, Tessa told herself. *Don't think about the war.*

It had been going on her entire life, her parents' entire lives, her grandparents' entire lives. The oldest person Tessa had ever heard of—Mr. Singleton from the first floor—was more than seventy, and even he didn't remember a time before the war. It was always there, as ever-present as air. The most talented children were selected for the military academies and sent away by the time they were ten; only rarely did any of them ever come back. But even people who weren't directly involved in the fighting were part of the war. They assembled bombs in factories; they packed food for the soldiers; they scavenged parts from damaged fighter planes.

For a moment Tessa felt like she could see the way the war weighed on everyone walking by in the darkness. People walked bent over, crouched down, defensive—looking defeated just by all the years of fighting. One figure in particular practically clutched the building, as if ready to dart in at the first sign of danger. Every few steps he'd whip his head around, as if every noise spooked him. Between steps he stood with his entire body tensed, watching.

That's Gideon, Tessa thought. *He's escaping.*

At this distance, with all the shadows, she couldn't see his face, could barely even make out his form. But she was still certain. Maybe it was because he was the only person on the sidewalk who didn't move groggily, in a stupor—with all the other people, she could tell that whatever pain they were in had been with them for so long they were numb to it.

Gideon moved as though his pain were fresh and raw and throbbing. He moved like a dying animal leaving a trail of blood behind it.

I can help him/I can stop him echoed in Tessa's brain, but fainter now. He didn't want anything to do with her. She held up the note again, and the words—*Forget about me. . . . Destroy . . . then there will be nothing to link . . .*—jumped out at her. She flicked her gaze back and forth between the note and the movements out in the darkness, Gideon edging farther and farther away from her. In a few moments he would be gone, and whatever other choices she had would be lost.

Gideon was at the corner now, peeking around the other side of the apartment building. As soon as he turned his head, one of the figures behind him on the sidewalk hustled forward. Gideon glanced back over his shoulder, and the suddenly energetic figure dived down, out of sight.

Gideon resumed walking, and the figure darted forward again, hiding only when Gideon glanced back a second time.

Gideon was being followed.

The indecision of *I have to help him/I have to stop him/He doesn't want me* melted away, swept out by a new resolve:

I have to warn him.

CHAPTER

10

Tessa burst out onto the street, having clattered down the stairs as fast as she could. With her first step out onto the pavement, she reminded herself to be careful; she couldn't call attention to herself here. She slipped into the crowd and slowed her pace to match the slow plodding of the people around her. It was maddening to do this—she wanted to run.

Maybe they're both gone, anyhow, Gideon and the one following him. . . .

But, no. A hooded head ducked down quickly, half a block ahead of Tessa, and she knew that that had to be the follower. She stood on tiptoes and saw, far ahead where the street sloped down, another head turn. If only there were more light, maybe she could have seen a flash of golden hair. But it wasn't just the streetlights that were out; it looked like the electricity was out on the first floor of their apartment building, too.

Strange, Tessa thought, creeping forward.

She peered around and saw that other lights were missing too: the tiny glow of red that always shone in the security cameras atop the apartment door. She'd *never* known those to be out. Did that mean the cameras weren't working?

Even stranger, Tessa thought.

She couldn't stop to figure it out. She concentrated on keeping the darting figure ahead of her in sight. She advanced one block, then two.

What good does this do? Tessa despaired. *I can't get past the follower to warn Gideon. Maybe I should run over to one of the parallel streets and get ahead of both of them?*

Just then, far ahead, Gideon turned a corner. He might start darting in a zigzag pattern now; he might go anywhere. If Tessa tried to run ahead on a parallel street, she might lose him.

So I just . . . watch?

Some of the old books Tessa had gotten from her grandparents' apartment had been spy novels. Tessa didn't think anyone made such things now, but she'd read lots of the old ones. The stories were full of spies tailing one another, and double agents taking advantage of the element of surprise.

That's what I have on my side, Tessa thought. *If the follower tries to do anything to Gideon, I'll run up to them and make a big scene, and Gideon will be able to get away.*

Tessa's heart pounded at the thought of the immense courage that would require. But she kept going, farther and farther from home, darting around corners behind the follower, behind Gideon.

Nothing to link you, Tessa remembered from Gideon's note, but it did seem they were linked now, all three of them: Gideon to the follower and the follower to Tessa, every bit as distinctly as if they were clinging to a rope slung between them.

The areas around them grew dodgier. Tessa lived in a bad neighborhood, an ugly neighborhood, but it was mostly that way just because of neglect. The people in her neighborhood had given up. In the buildings she passed now, the decay and decrepitude seemed like an active thing, a violence lurking in the air. There were smashed windows, gaping holes in walls, burn marks on bricks, abandoned factories with obscenities scrawled on every surface.

The crowds thinned out too, all the evil intent and despair distilled into a smaller and smaller number of people. Tessa shivered and drew the hood of her sweatshirt farther up, partially hiding her face. She hunched over slightly, trying to disguise the fact that she was a girl.

"Well, look at you," someone said, the innocent words laced with such menace that they seemed to be saying something else entirely.

Tessa flinched.

Gideon would come to my rescue if I cried out, wouldn't he? she wondered. And then she was disgusted with herself, because wasn't she there to rescue *him*? Was she so helpless that she couldn't survive someone speaking to her?

Automatically, she glanced ahead, scanning the crowd for another glimpse of Gideon.

Gideon was gone.

Tessa almost gasped, but the follower didn't seem puzzled.

The follower scurried three steps forward and then darted into a dark alley.

I am a fool, Tessa thought, and stepped blindly after the others.

Tessa stood for a moment at the edge of the alleyway, hoping her eyes would adjust. When they didn't—when the darkness before her stayed inky and indecipherable—her brain threw something at her from one of those old spy novels she'd read.

It's not like the street behind me is all that bright, but anyone looking out from this alley would see my silhouette. . . .

She dropped down to the ground, her hands and knees landing in a puddle. She told herself it was only water, but that was probably too much to hope for. She stayed low and listened, her ears straining to make up for everything she couldn't see.

She heard voices. First Gideon's, tight and almost angry: "That was the price we agreed on."

Then a stranger's, low and indistinct.

Tessa edged closer, deeper into the darkness. She moved slowly, her hands sweeping out before her. Her fingers brushed sleek, curved metal—the side of some sort of vehicle. In this part of the city she would have expected rusted fenders, smashed-up bumpers. But this vehicle, whatever it was, didn't seem to have so much as a dent.

"I know what I'm doing," Gideon said, the anger almost palpable in his voice.

Tessa thought that he and whoever he was talking to—the follower? Someone else?—were probably several feet away. She couldn't get too close for fear of running into one of them in the darkness.

Footsteps sounded, coming back toward Tessa.

Desperately, Tessa felt down lower on the side of the vehicle. Maybe she could hide underneath it. Lower, lower . . . her fingers hit some sort of latch, and a door slid open with a tiny whoosh of air.

The footsteps were getting closer.

You don't have the slightest idea what's going on here, Tessa's brain screamed at her. *It's something dangerous—hide!*

Tessa slipped in through the open door. She felt a seat before her—a leather seat, maybe?—and she scooted past it. She felt around, discovering a wide, flat, open space behind the seat. Maybe this was a van? Then Tessa found a padded column in the open space, and she shifted over to crouch on the other side of that.

Just in time, too, because the next time she heard the voices, they seemed to be coming from the open doorway.

"I know how to operate it perfectly well," Gideon said.

There was a soft thump—Gideon stepping into the vehicle?

"We'd hate to see you destroy your investment," the stranger replied, and this time he was close enough that Tessa could understand every word. His voice was oily and untrustworthy. "We have your best interest at heart."

Gideon snorted.

"I didn't pay you enough for that," he muttered.

Something clicked, and the barest amount of light glowed from near the seat in the front. Tessa huddled lower. Her foot touched something soft—a blanket?—and she pulled it over herself.

There was another soft click—the door closing. Tessa

listened hard, desperate to know if the stranger had been sealed inside or outside. But no more voices spoke.

The floor vibrated softly beneath Tessa, as some sort of engine purred to life. The vehicle moved—forward at first, and then, as it went faster and faster, not just forward but also . . .

Up.

For a moment Tessa couldn't make sense of this. *Up? How could we be going up?* Surely her senses were scrambled; surely she was just confused.

But she felt herself rising and rising and rising, along with the forward motion, and finally her brain supplied an explanation: *Oh. This isn't a car or a van. It's a plane.*

Of course, she had never been in a plane in her life. She'd never even seen one up close, only in pictures and news footage: the proud military jets soaring through the sky, defending the border. The helicopters ferrying military officials into or out of danger. The bombers speeding off toward the enemy lands . . .

Gideon flew a bomber in the war, Tessa remembered.

Could this be a bomber they were flying in now? Was he headed off on some secret military mission?

Tessa remembered the flat way Gideon had said, *I killed one thousand six hundred and thirty-two people. Do you still think I'm a hero?* She remembered the devastated look in his eyes. She couldn't imagine him dropping any more bombs.

Then where were they going? What was he doing?

Tessa couldn't think of any possible answers to either of those questions. It was too hard to think with all the weird forces of flight tugging at her: the floor rising beneath her, lifting her higher and higher, even as gravity seemed to be trying harder and harder to pull her back down. Then everything tilted, and she slid backward. She grabbed for something to hold on to, but there was nothing within her grasp except the blanket, which was sliding too.

"Oh, yeah!" Gideon cried from the front of the plane. "I know how to fly!"

Nobody answered him. Did that mean that the other man was still down below, back on the ground?

The blanket had slipped off Tessa's head, so she dared to look up. As far as Tessa could tell, Gideon was sitting in front of a dimly lit instrument panel. She couldn't see anyone in the copilot's seat beside him, but from this angle only a very tall, very large man would be visible.

She had to know if Gideon was alone or not.

Using the column and the wall as a support, Tessa clawed her way up to a standing position. She swayed unsteadily with the jerking and tilting of the plane.

"Turbulence?" Gideon muttered. "Or—are there still some external controls I need to override? What's hidden in the coding?"

He began frantically pressing buttons and pulling on controls. A computer screen glowed to life above the instrument panel, providing more light. But Gideon was flashing through various commands so quickly that the light was there and gone one instant to the next.

Tessa glimpsed a shape in the copilot's seat, but it was too small to be a person. Was it a backpack, maybe? A duffel bag? She rose on her tiptoes, wanting to be sure—

And the plane lurched to the side, slamming Tessa against a window.

"Oh, no! You are not in control anymore!" Gideon screamed from the pilot's seat. "This is my plane now!"

Tessa decided this probably wasn't the best time to spring forward and announce, *Guess what? I'm coming with you!* She found a strap to hang on to beneath the window, and clung to it for dear life. She realized she'd had her eyes squeezed shut ever since the plane had tilted sideways. But the jerking movement seemed to have stopped for the moment, so Tessa dared to open her eyes again.

The entire city lay beneath her.

And for now, for once, it was *beautiful.* The darkness hid all the dirt and despair and desperation. Under the night sky the city's lights stood out like gleaming jewels. The streetlights were lined up like beads on a necklace; glowing windows crowned the skyline. Tessa stared in amazement, her awe too great for her even to gasp. And then, as the city receded, the lights blurred into one another, all the patterns growing clear. It was a broken pattern, the string of streetlights missing entirely in one section of the city.

It was the same section where the bottom of every building stood in darkness.

Is that where Gideon and the follower and I were walking? she wondered. *Is it possible the lights went out only in that one area? Why? Was it on purpose? Who did that?*

These were more questions Tessa couldn't answer.

At the front of the plane Gideon was screaming even louder.

"No! No! Override!"

The plane dipped and swooped wildly, the window under Tessa's cheek spinning to show her the sky, the city, the sky, the city, each view little more than a flash before it vanished. And then the plane lurched, and the hand strap Tessa was holding on to was jerked from her grasp. She plunged backward, falling, falling, falling . . .

She landed, hitting hard. Her head struck the corner of something—a handle? A partially open door?

And then everything went black.

CHAPTER

12

Tessa woke to light.

She was bathed in it, swimming in it—it was the most glorious light she'd ever seen. Even with her eyes still closed, she could feel it teasing against her eyelids: *Wake up! Rise up! It's such a bright world out here!*

Tessa opened her eyes.

For a moment she was too sun-dazzled to actually see anything. But then her eyes focused on something in the light: Gideon.

He had his white uniform on again, and Tessa tried groggily to remember if he might have been wearing that last night and she just hadn't noticed. But he was bent over the copilot's seat, as if tidying up, and Tessa figured out what must have happened.

He was wearing other clothes last night. He had the uniform in his duffel bag or backpack or whatever he carried onto the plane. He changed while I was . . . sleeping.

Tessa was still trying to put together everything that had happened the night before: the darkness, the follower, Gideon's conversation with the oily-voiced man, the crazily swooping plane. It was still too hard to make sense of, too hard to reconcile the darkness and the screaming of the night before with this glowing vision before her eyes now: Gideon in his uniform.

Tessa wanted to say something, to get Gideon to turn around and notice her. But even in the sunlight she wouldn't be gleaming. She could feel something caked in her hair—blood?—and her face felt puffy and bruised. She looked down and saw that both her sweatshirt and her ragged jeans were streaked with mud.

She remembered what she'd been called the last time she'd seen Gideon in his uniform: *gnat . . . flea . . . slug . . .* Tessa calling out to Gideon now would be like a gnat trying to speak to a god.

Gideon smoothed down his already perfect hair. Tessa realized the plane had stopped moving; everything was still. In the absence of any other motion or sound, Tessa was acutely aware of Gideon taking a deep breath. His shoulders rose, resolutely. He did not let the breath back out right away. Instead he took a single step toward the door and hit a switch.

The door slid open, the light pouring over Tessa in even greater abundance. How could Gideon not see her now? But he wasn't looking in her direction. He was standing in the doorway, facing out into the blinding light.

Tessa saw him take another deep breath.

"I am sorry," he said in a booming voice. Tessa's eyes were too light-dazed to see who he was speaking to.

Gideon kept talking.

"I came to apologize. You can arrest me, kill me—punish me however you see fit. I am the one who killed your countrymen in this place. . . ."

In a flash Tessa understood.

Gideon had flown them into enemy territory.

He'd flown them to the very spot where he'd killed all those people.

He was willing to be killed too.

No—he was asking for it.

Tessa's body reacted as quickly as her mind. Before she was even conscious of moving, she was already on her feet and running toward Gideon. Her legs tangled in the blanket, but she kept going, diving for Gideon. She knocked him sideways onto the floor of the plane, so if any of the enemy were already trying to shoot him, the bullets would just whiz harmlessly past. But this wasn't enough. It wasn't enough to tackle him, to hold him down, the mud from her ragged clothes rubbing off on his spotless white uniform. Guns could be reloaded, re-aimed, fired again and again and again.

Tessa rose up and slammed her hand against the control on the wall.

The door slid shut.

CHAPTER

13

"What? Who? But . . . *Tessa*?" Gideon said. His eyes focused on her face, and he wailed, "Noooo . . . Now I'm going to be responsible for your death too!"

He curled inward, almost in the same pose of despair Tessa had seen him in that day she'd taken him flowers.

"No one's going to die," Tessa said, with more confidence than she felt. "Not me, not you—you're going to get us out of here!"

For a moment Gideon didn't move, and Tessa had to tug him toward the pilot's seat.

"Fly!" she commanded.

Gideon looked at her again, and he seemed to snap to, scrambling into the pilot's seat under his own power.

"Yes, yes, I have to try," he mumbled. "I can't let . . ."

He didn't even bother finishing the sentence. He was a flurry of motion, hitting levers, punching buttons, tapping the computer screen.

Tessa cast an anxious glance toward the door she'd just slammed shut. She expected it to spring open again any minute now and reveal a cluster of evil-looking soldiers pointing guns at her and Gideon. She stumbled over toward the switch she'd hit before.

"Is there any way to lock—"

"It's locked *now*," Gideon snapped at her. "Get down! The window—"

Tessa ducked.

There were actually two windows: the one she'd had her face pressed against the night before, and another one on the other side of the plane, directly across from it. Those windows were the source of the light that had wakened Tessa so dramatically only a few moments ago. But, from this angle, she couldn't really see out of them now. Tessa would have expected a third window at the front of the plane, so the pilot could see out to fly, but the computer screen lay there instead.

The computer screen showed only words: *System not engaged. Troubleshoot?*

Tessa didn't like to see the word "shoot," even on a computer screen. Then the real meaning of the message sank in: For some reason, the plane wasn't springing back to life, soaring back into the air.

Tessa cast another fearful glance at the two windows behind her.

If the door is locked, the enemy will come in through one of those windows, Tessa thought. *They'll smash in with their guns, and Gideon and I will have to defend ourselves. . . .*

"Do you have any weapon in that backpack of yours?" Tessa asked tensely. "Or should I look in that closet back there—?"

Tessa pointed toward the rear of the plane, to the door handle she'd smashed her head against the night before. There seemed to be a tiny closet or cupboard built into the wall of the plane.

Gideon grabbed Tessa's arm and yanked her down lower.

"Don't go anywhere near those windows!" he commanded.

"But—," Tessa began. She realized Gideon wasn't listening. He was peering at the computer screen in horror.

"Why won't the engine work?" he muttered. "Override! Override!"

"What's wrong?" Tessa asked.

He flashed her a look of deep frustration.

"I don't know!" he screamed.

He began hitting buttons again, typing in commands. The view on the screen changed rapidly, one screen shot after another, but nothing seemed to give Gideon the information he wanted.

"I'll have to tap into the overall system," he muttered. His hands flew over the keys, code flashing across the screen. Tessa lost track of the number of times he was asked to provide a password.

And then Gideon stopped moving. He just sat, staring at the screen. The color drained from his face.

"No," he moaned. "No. Not this."

"*What?*" Tessa demanded.

"There's been . . . a disabling signal sent out," Gideon whispered.

Tessa tried to absorb this.

Be brave, she told herself.

"Well, you really can't blame the enemy for doing that," she said, and the calmness in her own voice amazed her.

"It's not the enemy sending out that signal," Gideon said. There was enough horror in his voice for both of them.

"Not the enemy?" Tessa asked. "But—"

"It's our own country," Gideon explained.

On the screen a wavy line flickered. Tessa guessed this showed the frequency of the disabling signal.

"Our own country?" Tessa repeated, confused. "Then—can't you just ask them to stop?"

"No," Gideon whispered. "Because . . . You need to see this so you'll know . . . so you can decide how to spend your last moments. . . ."

He typed something, and the view on the screen changed. Now there were blips of light that seemed to be flying in formation toward an X at the bottom of the screen.

"This is how our military does things," Gideon murmured. Just listening to the pain in his voice was agonizing. "We always send out a disabling signal before a bombing run."

"*Bombing* run?" Tessa repeated numbly.

"Yes," Gideon said, his voice like a sob. With one trembling finger he traced the blips of light on the screen. "It's an entire fleet of bombers—they're only seconds away from their target." Now his finger brushed the X at the bottom of the screen. "And their target? We're right in the middle of it."

CHAPTER

14

"I'm so sorry," Gideon said, and now he was sobbing.

Tessa rose up from the floor and grabbed Gideon's shoulders.

"Stop that," she hissed, shaking him. "Stop apologizing and stop *them*."

She jabbed her finger toward the blips of light on the screen.

"You can contact them and let them know we're here," she said. "They won't bomb us. They'll . . . rescue us."

Tessa liked this idea. It had sprung into her mind fully formed, a beautiful thing. She could see planeloads of men in uniforms like Gideon's storming in, fending off hordes of enemy troops, carrying Tessa and Gideon to safety.

She couldn't understand why Gideon, who was supposed to be so brilliant, hadn't thought of it first.

But Gideon was shaking his head violently.

"I already tried that," he moaned. "It won't work without hours of tampering. This is a stolen plane. All the tracking links were erased—I erased some of them myself. Any signal we send out will look like a decoy, the enemy attempting to impersonate one of our jets. . . ." Gideon grabbed Tessa's hand back from the computer and pressed it against his tear-stained face.

"I'm so sorry," he whispered again. "So sorry, so, so sorry . . ."

Tessa stood frozen, her hand on Gideon's face. On the computer screen the blips of light drew closer and closer to the X. Little dotted lines dropped down from the blips.

"Those are the bombs," Gideon murmured. "Forgive me!"

He sprang from his pilot's seat, knocking Tessa flat against the ground. He cowered over her, and dimly Tessa realized that he was trying to protect her, trying to make sure that, if anyone survived the next few moments, it would be her.

I should have left my parents a note last night, she thought vaguely. *I should have . . .*

The word that blossomed in her mind was "lived." She should have lived a better life, a fuller life, a more meaningful life, while she'd still had the chance.

"It's okay," she told Gideon. If there'd been more time, she would have explained what that meant: that she didn't regret following him the night before. That the best moment of her life had actually been saving him—*trying* to save him—only a few minutes ago when she'd tackled him and slammed the door. At least she'd gotten a little taste of life before going to her death. Of heroism, even. A taste of being something more than a slug or a gnat or a flea.

If there'd been more time, there was so much she would have wanted to say to Gideon. But there wasn't more time. Gideon was burying his face against her collarbone, and counting off under his breath, "Three, two, one . . ."

Tessa threw her arms around Gideon and held on tight.

15

Zero, Tessa counted off in her mind. She flinched, expecting explosions and flames and everything falling in on her.

Nothing happened.

Um . . . zero . . . now? she thought, still flinching, still holding on to Gideon for dear life. It figured that Tessa was so pathetic that she couldn't even time a countdown correctly, that she finished with her noble, dying thoughts too soon and had to have one of her last thoughts be, *Um*.

Still nothing happened.

Tessa relaxed her flinch a little and tilted her head back. She could see the sunlight still streaming peacefully in through the window, lighting up the gold in Gideon's hair.

He was still holding on to her, still sobbing against her shoulder, "My fault, all my fault . . ."

If there's anything left of us to find after we're dead, Tessa thought, *people will think this is so romantic, us dying in each other's arms.*

But it wasn't actually romantic. It was awkward and uncomfortable and slightly embarrassing to be lying there like that, Gideon blubbering out his apologies.

And somehow Tessa had stopped believing that they were about to die.

Tessa pushed gently against Gideon's chest, pushing him away.

"Um, Gideon?" she said hesitantly. "Do you think maybe you might have been . . . wrong?"

He stopped apologizing and lifted his head and looked at her, confused.

"Look," Tessa said, pointing toward one of the windows. "See any bombs?"

Gideon stared at her a moment longer.

"But—"

He shook his head and scrambled up, back into the pilot's seat.

"You must have been wrong about the target's location," Tessa offered. "You were in a hurry. It's easy to make a mistake at a time like that."

"I was trained," Gideon said through gritted teeth, "to never make mistakes. *Especially* not when I'm in a hurry."

He was back to typing and tapping. Tessa crouched beside him and watched. The computer seemed to have gone into sleep mode, but Gideon brought it back to life. He froze the picture of the blips of light and the bombs falling over the X, and then he clicked on the X to get exact geographical coordinates. Then he moved that picture to the side of the screen and called up another image: the start of the video Tessa had first seen on her own computer in Gideon's room, the one showing the bombs falling over the marketplace, with the mothers and children and babies dying on the ground. He froze this image as well and circled the numbers at the bottom that Tessa had ignored before. She stared at the numbers now and figured out what they were: the geographical coordinates of that bombing.

"That was why I needed to watch the video before, back at my mother's place," Gideon muttered. "I needed to memorize the coordinates."

"Okay, okay, maybe *this* place and *this* place are the same," Tessa argued, pointing at each side of the screen as she studied the numbers. They were identical. "But you must be wrong about where *we* are."

Gideon opened up a smaller portion of the screen, and typed in *Give exact coordinates of this plane.*

A lengthy string of numbers showed up on this portion of the screen. Gideon circled all the numbers and enlarged them, stacking them one on top of the other. All three sets matched exactly, down to five decimal places.

"Satisfied?" Gideon asked in a harsh voice.

Tessa shook her head. She touched the dotted lines frozen mid-fall from the blips of light on the computer screen.

"Then these aren't bombs," she said. "Or—they were all duds. Empty casings."

She was proud of herself for coming up with this explanation. There were rumors sometimes, back in Waterford City, about how the stories the military told about their glorious victories couldn't all be true. "If they were, don't you think we'd have won the whole war by now, not just a battle here and there?" some people argued.

Gideon enlarged the bombing image so that it overshadowed the trio of matching numbers. He unfroze the image, letting the footage advance.

"T minus three," he intoned. "T minus two. T minus one . . ."

On the screen the dotted lines streamed down to the X marking the target. Then the screen blanked out momentarily before flashing the words *Direct hit! Direct hit! Direct hit!*

"See?" Gideon said. He began typing in yet another flurry of numbers and letters, bringing up even more indecipherable code. Though, now that she was watching more carefully, Tessa noticed that the code always included the geographical coordinates Gideon had shown her earlier.

"All the data in the entire military system shows that we were incinerated three minutes ago," Gideon insisted, returning to the same screenfuls of information again and again. "Everything shows that!"

"Except that we're still alive," Tessa murmured.

She glanced over her shoulder and confirmed that the sunlight was still streaming in the window. From this angle she couldn't see much else, but—was that shadow a tree branch swaying gently in the breeze? Was that faint chirping she could hear actually *birdsong*?

Tessa tapped one of the minimized portions of the computer screen, the stopped footage of the people dying in the marketplace.

"Show me the video like this of the bombing that you say just hit us," she said. "The video with all the details. Then we'll see what really happened."

"I can't," Gideon said. "That always comes a day or two late, because it's from spy satellites and we only get the downloads every other day. That's why . . ." He was staring at the screen, at the image of the marketplace a moment before the bombs hit, when everyone was screaming and running as if they actually had a chance to escape. "That's why I was so happy, at first, when I found out how many people I'd killed. It was . . . kind of a record for a single pilot, in a single day, and everybody was slapping me on the back and punching me on the arm and congratulating me. . . . I didn't think of it as *people,* you know?" He touched the screen lightly, his fingers practically caressing the faces before him. "Not babies, not children, not . . . not anyone it'd be wrong to kill."

"Couldn't you see any of that from your plane, flying overhead, right before you dropped the bombs?" Tessa asked, and she was surprised that her voice came out sounding so harsh.

Gideon flinched as if she'd hit him.

"I was never in that bomber," he said. "Pilots in the military always fly their planes remotely, from computers hundreds of miles away. We're sitting at a desk. We're *safe.* All we see is what the military wants us to see, the X where the target is and the blips of different-colored lights for our planes and the enemy's planes. That's how it always is. Didn't you know?"

Tessa thought about this. *Had* she known that? Everything about the military and the war was always so vague and far away. So, "Look, everyone! Look at your great hero, Gideon

Thrall!" Not, "Look, everyone! Wouldn't you like to see and hear what he really did?"

Her face twisted. She'd fallen for it too. Back at the awards ceremony she'd admired Gideon as much as anyone.

She'd admired his "courage," when all he'd done was sit at a desk playing a video game.

A game that killed people.

"Don't feel bad," Gideon said softly, clearly misinterpreting her grimace. "It's not exactly a secret how things are done, but the military likes to make it sound like we're always flying off into danger, risking our lives to protect everyone else. . . ."

Tessa glared at him.

"Let me get this straight," she said. "Had you ever actually even flown a plane before last night? A plane you were sitting in for real?"

Gideon bit his lip and shook his head.

"No," he admitted.

"Then the only brave thing you ever did in your entire life was the way you were trying to commit suicide?" Tessa asked.

Gideon gaped at her.

"Not *suicide*," he protested. "Not that. I was trying to . . . make amends. Atone. There was no other way. I couldn't undo what I did. I couldn't bring anybody back to life. So I thought the closest thing I could do to making everything right was just to . . . apologize."

"And then you expected the enemy to kill you," Tessa said. "I heard what you said! You were asking to be punished!"

Her head spun. Her stomach churned. This was a

nightmare. She'd *believed* in him. In that moment that she'd dived for him and shut the door, she'd believed completely that he was still noble and true and heroic. That even if she took a bullet intended for him, it would be worth it. She wouldn't have minded sacrificing her own life for his.

But now . . . she didn't know what to make of the bombing raid that the computer insisted had just happened. She didn't know what would happen next. But she had definitely put herself in danger for Gideon. She'd risked her life for him.

And he'd never been anything but a fake.

"Tessa," Gideon said pleadingly, and it was like he was asking her to look at him the way she'd looked at him before, when she'd idolized him.

"I'm going to die because of you," Tessa said. "For no reason. For *nothing*."

Something rattled behind them, and Tessa realized how foolish they'd been, talking about bombs that hadn't actually fallen, about a massacre that had happened ages ago—when both of them were in danger *now*. It probably hadn't been more than ten or fifteen minutes since Gideon had stood in the door of the airplane asking someone to kill him. He'd just gotten a ten-minute reprieve, while the enemy gathered their forces, plotted their strategies . . .

Tessa whirled around, her eyes quickly scanning the door and both windows. Maybe there was still some hope. If the enemy was trying to get in through the window on the left, maybe she and Gideon could escape through the door to the right.

But as far as Tessa could tell, there wasn't anyone trying

to get in through the door or either of the windows. Instead the handle of the closet door was jerking up and down, on its own, as if by magic.

That was the source of the rattling noise.

"Where does that lead to?" Tessa hissed at Gideon. "Outside?"

He didn't answer. He was already jumping from his seat and scrambling toward the closet, his hand stretched out toward the handle. He clearly planned to hold it shut, his brute strength keeping out whoever was on the other side.

He was too late. The door sprang open, swinging outward.

And then someone rolled out from behind the door: a kid. A kid who was all big eyes in a too-thin face, mostly hidden behind spikily cut dark hair and ragged clothes. The kid blinked, the outsized eyes taking in the sight of Gideon standing over her and Tessa looming nearby.

"Oh, crud," the kid said. "You were supposed to be gone by now."

16

"Who are you?" Tessa asked.

"Whose side are you on?" Gideon asked.

"Where did you come from?" Tessa asked.

"What were you doing in that closet?" Gideon asked.

"What do you mean we were supposed to be gone by now?" Tessa asked.

The kid didn't answer either of them. Tessa saw the kid's gaze flicker from Gideon to Tessa to the door to the windows . . . to the pilot's seat.

Gideon must have noticed this too.

"Do you know how to reset the plane for flying, when it's been disabled?" he asked. He glared at her. "Were you the one who disabled it?"

The kid's eyes kept darting about.

"Why aren't you outside checking out the engine, to see why it isn't working?" the kid said. "People *always* go out to check the engine."

"Not in enemy territory," Tessa said drily.

Tessa wouldn't have thought it possible, but the kid's eyes got even bigger.

"What?" the kid asked. "Where *are* we?"

She sprang up and dashed toward the pilot's seat.

"Keep down!" Gideon commanded. "You don't want anyone to see you through the windows!"

The kid had already dropped into a rolling position to get past the windows.

I think she knows more than Gideon and I do about staying out of sight, Tessa thought.

There was something familiar about the kid's nervous, jerky movements. Suddenly Tessa knew why.

"It was you!" she burst out. "You were the one following Gideon last night!"

"What?" Gideon asked.

"Someone was following you, all the way from the apartment building to that dark alley where you got the plane," Tessa said. "That's why *I* started following you, because I was going to warn you—"

"When were you planning to tell me that?" Gideon asked.

"Well, we've been a little bit busy," Tessa said sarcastically. "Anyhow, once you started talking to that man in the alley, I thought it was just him who'd been following you. Obviously, you knew he was there."

"You mean Rondo?" the kid asked, as she eased into the

pilot's seat. "You think Rondo would do his own surveillance? Never! He might actually have to break a sweat!"

Gideon looked at Tessa as soon as the kid's back was turned. If Tessa hadn't just decided she was completely disillusioned with Gideon, she would have been thrilled by that look, because it was so conspiratorial. It clearly said, *I trust you. I don't trust this kid. We're partners against her, all right?*

Tessa flashed a look back at Gideon. She hoped he could read her thoughts in her face: *Look, that kid weighs maybe seventy pounds. I think either one of us could overpower her if we had to. Why don't we pretend to go along with whatever she says, and see if she can actually get the plane working again?*

Aloud, Tessa said, "Then . . . if you've been on this plane since back in Waterford City, you're probably not one of the enemy. Are you?"

"Doesn't seem logical, does it?" the kid agreed. "If I were the enemy, why would I bother infiltrating Eastam, just to secretly fly back with you to . . . oh, crap! We really are in the war zone!" She'd refreshed the computer screen and was staring at the same geographical coordinates Gideon had called up before. "I was hoping you were just too stupid to read the navigational data, but it turns out you're even bigger fools than I thought. Why in the world would you have . . ." She was turning around in her seat to face them, and suddenly shouted, "Get down!"

Automatically, Tessa and Gideon dropped to the floor.

"Where are they coming from?" Gideon asked in a tense whisper. "Where's the attack?"

The kid rolled her eyes side to side, glancing toward each window.

"There's no attack yet, that I can see," she said, and now her voice was hushed and urgent too. "That was mostly just a precaution. Testing your reflexes. You don't know the angle anyone could be looking from, through those windows. We've got to go into desperado mode. I want to get out of here alive, so it's probably a package deal. I'll have to keep the two of you alive too."

"That would be . . . nice," Tessa said faintly. She had rug burn on her cheek now, along with the bruises from falling last night.

Gideon had begun crawling on his elbows toward the front of the plane, so Tessa decided to do the same.

"Look," Gideon said. "I'm a military pilot. I know how to—"

The kid cut him off with a snort.

"The fact you ended up here, that's pretty much proof you don't know squat," she said. She snorted again. "Military pilots! Bunch of pampered, overfed desk jockeys, think they know how to fly . . ."

"He flew here on purpose," Tessa said, because even though she was disillusioned with Gideon, she didn't think he deserved quite that much scorn.

"Why?" the kid asked.

"To apologize," Gideon said. "I . . . killed a lot of people here last year."

"What—you wanted to visit their graves? You thought they were going to be able to hear you?" the kid asked. She had her head tilted to the side, sneaking glances toward the windows.

"No—I was going to apologize to the survivors," Gideon said.

"You did apologize," Tessa said. Once again she felt like she needed to defend him. She looked back at the kid. "He stood right in the doorway, and announced everything he'd done, and asked for punishment. . . ."

"You had the door open?" the kid asked, snapping her attention back from the windows and leaning closer to Tessa and Gideon. "What did you see outside?"

Tessa was annoyed with herself that she hadn't thought to ask that question a long time ago.

Believing you're about to die . . . it kind of makes it hard to think straight, she told herself.

Gideon winced.

"I didn't actually see anything," he admitted. "I kind of . . . had my eyes shut. I just thought a military plane with the enemy's insignia on the outside . . . it was bound to attract attention. . . ."

"So we don't know what's going on outside," the kid said. "You disabled the exterior cameras last night, and it's going to take another minute or two for them to cycle back on. So we don't know if it's going to be safer to restart the engines right now, or if it's safer to wait until dark. Do we have enough fuel to get back home?"

"I didn't think I'd need—," Gideon began.

"Never mind," the kid said. "I don't want to slow the computer down by checking data like that in the overall system right now. But there's a manual fuel gauge in that closet. Works even when the engine's been disabled." A mischievous look danced over her face, almost as if she were enjoying herself. "Could one of you go see what it says?"

Gideon and Tessa looked at each other.

"I will," Gideon said, and began crawling back toward the closet.

The kid motioned for Tessa to crawl closer to the pilot's seat.

Is this a trap? Tessa wondered. *Would I be a fool to trust her?*

She reminded herself that the kid was scrawny and undersized, and that Gideon was nearby. What did she expect the kid to do?

She lurched forward.

"What you have to ask yourself," the kid said in a low voice that Gideon probably wouldn't be able to hear from back at the closet, "is why he made that choice. Is he protecting you? Or did he pick what he thought was the safer job for himself?"

"Or," Tessa said, "was he just not sure I'd be able to read a manual fuel gauge?"

The kid raised an eyebrow in surprise.

"Ah," she said. "You're someone who tries to consider all the possibilities. I like that. Might come in handy getting us out of here." She stuck out her hand. "I'm Dek."

Tessa shook it.

"Tessa," she said. She tilted her head backward. "And he's Gideon Thrall."

Tessa had kind of expected the name to make an impact on Dek, but Dek's expression didn't change.

"He your boyfriend?" she asked.

Tessa hesitated.

"No," she said.

"Good," Dek said. "Never fall in love with one of those ex-military types. Sometimes their brains are a little scrambled. And I'd say he's showing all the signs." She pointed over her shoulder, back toward Gideon.

It annoyed Tessa that Dek could sound so world-weary and wise when she didn't even look like she'd passed her tenth birthday. Tessa wanted to defend Gideon again, but she couldn't exactly say he'd been acting normal.

"How do you know he's *ex*-military?" Tessa challenged instead.

"One, he just bought a stolen military plane on the black market," Dek said. "And, two, he flew it into enemy territory. If he wasn't ex-military before, he's ex-military now."

Tessa opened her mouth to respond to that. She wanted to change the subject. What could she say to tease out more information about Dek and Dek's reasons for stowing away on the plane?

How does she know this is a stolen, black-market airplane? Tessa wondered. *Is she pretty much admitting that she works for the black marketers?*

Just then the entire plane shuddered. Something had rammed into it. Tessa jerked her head to the right, half expecting to see a gaping hole in the side. The wall still looked the same, but a moment later the plane shuddered again.

"Change of plans!" Dek screamed. She was simultaneously fastening a seat belt across her lap and stabbing frantically at the computer screen. "We're not waiting for the external cameras to come on! We are taking off now! Let's get out of here!"

17

The entire plane lurched to the side once more, almost rolling over. But then the engine zoomed to life. Dek *had* known how to revive it. She did something to rev it up, the almost inaudible hum of the night before replaced by a fearsome growl.

Gideon jumped back from the closet.

"No!" he shouted. "They'll hear us!"

"What—don't you think they already know we're here?" Dek screamed back at him. "We need as much power as we can get!"

"You'll have the whole country out here shooting at us!" Gideon yelled.

"You don't think that's going to happen anyway?" Dek yelled back.

The plane jerked forward. Tessa almost fell over backward, but caught the column at the last minute. Gideon slammed against the closet door.

"You don't have the external cameras working yet!" he screamed, squinting toward the computer screen in front of Dek. "You're flying blind!"

"Then look out the freaking window!" Dek screamed.

Objections flooded Tessa's mind: *What? You want to give the enemy something to shoot at instead of you?* And *If the whole country's going to be shooting at us, why even try?* And *Is this another of your tests? This is no time to check out how good our reflexes are, or whether Gideon is going to protect himself or me!*

Tessa stepped toward the window anyhow. It was a relief, finally, to look out, to stop imagining the horrendous enemies swarming toward her and just stare them down.

Tessa saw . . . trees.

She blinked, thinking, *How can the enemy be so good at hiding when they're attacking us?* She tilted her head this way and that. There. Off to the side, practically out of sight, a huge dark shape slammed against the tail end of the plane.

The whole plane shuddered again.

"It's a . . . buffalo? A moose?" Tessa guessed. She tried to remember pictures she'd seen in books. "Bison?"

The plane lurched forward, the engine grinding louder.

"Prepare for takeoff!" Dek screamed from the front.

Tessa grabbed the rim of the window, holding on as well as she could. The plane zigzagged, and Tessa got a better glimpse of the creature behind them.

"Definitely a moose!" she cried. "I see antlers!"

Gideon dived toward her, pressing his face against the glass too.

"So the enemy is using animatronic robots, disguised as ordinary wildlife," he muttered. "Could their robotics program be that far ahead of ours? I have to get back to HQ to tell them this!"

"I don't know," Tessa said doubtfully. "It looks real."

"Exactly," Gideon said.

"I mean . . . ," Tessa began, then gave up.

The plane lifted as it lurched forward, and the creature raised its head to watch. Tessa would have liked to just stand there and stare. The moose, if that's what it was, was so majestic, so . . . *extravagant* . . . the immense antlers unfurling so gracefully on either side of his head. This was a creature that wasn't afraid to take up a lot of space—in fact, it didn't seem to be afraid of anything.

Gideon shoved Tessa down, away from the window.

"They'll be shooting at us soon," he muttered. He turned his head toward Dek at the front of the plane. "*Please* tell me you've got the antiaircraft defense shields up!"

"Of course!" Dek snarled back at him. "*I* never disabled anything but the engine, and as you can hear, it's working now. You disabled, what? Forty separate systems? Fifty?"

"Only the ones that had your bosses' tracking codes embedded in them," Gideon muttered. "They must not trust you much, to have that much backup. What's the system—every time they sell a plane, you stow away, make it look like it's broken, and then steal it back?"

Tessa expected Dek to deny this, but she only shrugged.

"Usually the buyers are so rich and so drunk, it's kind of a safety precaution, getting the plane away from them," she said. "It's my way of making sure all the rich drunk guys stay alive so they can keep buying things from my bosses."

She sounded distracted, huddled over the instrument panel. She slammed her hand against her seat.

"Come on, cameras—now! We need you!"

The plane lurched to the side—automatically dodging antiaircraft fire? Automatically dodging something else? Or just . . . by mistake? Tessa didn't know enough about flying to be able to tell.

"You should let me take the controls," Gideon said, inching along the floor toward the pilot's seat. "To keep us all alive."

Dek didn't even look at him.

"In an emergency the rule is you let the most experienced pilot fly," she said. "And in this plane that's me. I've got hundreds of flying hours. *Real* flying hours."

Tessa expected Gideon to argue, but he didn't.

"You went to the military academy too," he said, watching Dek's scrawny hands dance over the instrument panel.

"Wrong," Dek corrected him. "I was *selected* for the military academy. Didn't go. There's a difference."

Gideon gasped.

"It's not a choice," he said. "You're selected to go, you go. Or else—"

"Or else you cease to exist," Dek finished for him. "So I ceased to exist. In the official records."

Tessa supposed she should feel good that both of the people on the plane with her were such geniuses that they'd been selected for the military academy. But it just made her feel even more dull and witless than usual.

And then she forgot all her inadequacies, because her body felt so weird. The plane rocked with the force of speeding faster, soaring higher, fighting the pull of gravity. Maybe Dek wasn't using the standard, approved method for taking off. Even more than the night before, Tessa felt plastered to the floor, tugged backward and down.

"Yes!" Dek shrieked. "The cameras are coming back on . . . right . . . now! So we'll see . . ." Suddenly she gasped. "What's that?"

18

Gideon and Tessa both struggled toward the front of the plane, toward Dek and the computer screen. Gideon got there first, but Tessa wasn't far behind.

Tessa pulled herself up on the side of the pilot's seat and squinted at the screen. It took her a moment to figure out what she was seeing. She was braced for a view of squadron after squadron of fighter planes circling them, firing off one shot after the other. But she saw no other planes around them at all.

Instead Dek was pointing to something on the ground, a huge U-shaped arc of metal that curved across a mighty river and had somehow cut a swath through a vast forest on the other side.

Now Gideon was gasping, too.

"It's the Santl Arch," he said. "It's . . . down?"

"Yes, down," Dek repeated. "Of course it's down! We're up, it's down—but what is it?"

Gideon seemed a little dazed.

"It was one of the enemy's most impressive feats of architecture," he said. "This must have just happened, that it fell. Last night before we got here or . . . I don't know. That was always a goal for fighter pilots, that if you did something great, you were allowed to fly through the arch. . . ."

"You mean, that thing used to be up in the air?" Tessa asked, because surely she wasn't understanding right.

"It was," Gideon said. "I flew through the center of it twice, as my victory lap, the night I ki—well, you know what I did."

Tessa was staring at the metal arch that looped below them with such awe that she almost missed noticing the way Gideon had said that. He'd stopped himself from saying the word "killed." Was he too ashamed? Or was he just trying not to remind Dek what he was capable of?

"You mean you flew through it twice *by remote*," Dek said scornfully. "You personally were hundreds of miles away. It was like you were flying a *toy*."

"Not a toy," Gideon said softly.

He was staring down at the computer screen with an expression Tessa couldn't read.

"So what's the military significance of knocking down that arch?" Dek said. "I'm guessing you think it was some of your fellow flyboys who did that."

"Yeah . . . ," Gideon said vaguely. He shook his head, as if trying to clear it. "Destruction of an enemy's beloved landmarks can have an intense psychological impact," he said, as if quoting. He kind of looked like the Santl Arch had been one of his beloved landmarks too. "And I'm sure there was a significant loss of life when it fell on . . . wait a minute! There wasn't a forest across the river from the arch! It was houses, factories, offices—buildings. Lots of buildings."

He reached down and enlarged the scene across the river, zooming in close.

"I don't understand," he said.

He began flipping through images all across the screen, zooming in, zooming out. Dek started to reach forward to stop him, but then she seemed to change her mind.

"Doesn't look right . . . No, not that . . . ," Gideon mumbled. "But the river's right! That *is* the Mighty Mysip! It's got to be! And the arch, only down . . ."

"Things look different when you're flying over them for *real*," Dek said smugly.

"But—," Gideon began.

Tessa didn't want the two of them getting into an argument.

"Um, could we maybe just focus on making sure no one's going to be shooting us?" Tessa asked nervously. "Could we plan how we're going to get out of here safely?"

"Oh, the shields are up," Dek said, almost sounding carefree.

"And no one from the enemy's forces is flying anywhere near us," Gideon said. He zoomed out even more than before, revealing a blue sky as far as the eye could see, above the ribbon of river winding through miles and miles of forest. "Now, how can that be?" he mumbled. "How is it that they didn't see us? That we can't see any of *them*? Where are they?"

"Maybe the enemy has replaced all its planes with hundreds of animatronic, robotic *trees*," Dek said. She giggled.

Gideon ignored her.

"This is all wrong," he murmured. "Really, really wrong." He furrowed his brows. "Let's fly to the north."

"Why?" Dek challenged.

"Well, for one thing, if you don't, we're going to run into the flight paths for *our* military's planes and spy satellites," Gideon said. "And, right now, in this aircraft, they wouldn't take to us any more kindly than the enemy would."

"Good point," Dek said. She made a couple adjustments, and the plane veered to the left.

Tessa felt the surge in speed in the pit of her stomach. For that matter her stomach also seemed sensitive to the sudden turn, to the tension between Gideon and Dek, and to the strain of thinking they were going to be shot any minute.

Dek began digging under the pilot's seat. She brought up a plastic-wrapped brown square and handed it to Tessa.

"Eat," Dek said. "It's never a good idea to fly on an empty stomach, though I bet fake-flyboy over there didn't know enough to tell you that." She tossed one toward Gideon as well, as if to soften the insult. "They're nutri-squares. Mass produced. They kind of taste like cardboard, but it's better than throwing up."

Tessa watched Gideon to see if he thought it was safe to take food from Dek. He absentmindedly peeled back the plastic and began chewing, so Tessa did the same. But Gideon was staring so fixedly at the computer screen that maybe he'd eat cardboard and never notice.

"Can't be," he murmured. "No . . . where's S-fiel? Pee-ore? Where are the houses? The farms? The people?"

"Can't see people when you're this high up," Dek told him.

"I know, I just . . ." Gideon scrunched up his face and went back to staring at the screen.

An alarm started buzzing from the instrument panel.

"Fuel supplies at critical levels," a mechanical voice spoke. "Locking in route toward nearest fueling source."

"No!" both Gideon and Dek screamed together. For a moment it almost seemed like they were working as a team, each of them stabbing at the controls and crying out, "Try the auto—"

"No, won't work. What about—"

"Still disabled—"

"Then—"

"That won't work either!"

It was like neither one of them needed to finish a sentence for the other to understand.

Tessa stood off to the side, feeling useless.

Then Dek let out a shriek, and Gideon moaned, and Tessa understood too.

They were going down.

CHAPTER

19

"We're going to crash!" Tessa screamed.

"Emergency non-pilot-controlled landing," Dek said, still with just a bit of swagger in her voice. "Not *quite* the same thing." She hit Gideon's shoulder. "Why didn't you check the fuel gauge when I told you to?"

"Because *you* insisted on taking off without going through any preflight check!" Gideon snarled back at her. "Remember?"

He was still stabbing at the controls, trying to get the plane to do something different.

"Hello? We were under attack!" Dek spat back. "If *you* hadn't turned off the external cameras—"

"Yeah, well, I would have thought *you* would have checked the computerized fuel gauge once we were in the air—"

"You disabled that, too, remember?"

"Would you two just shut up?" Tessa screamed. "What can we do *now* to get ready?"

Dek looked back at her and seemed to realize that Tessa was just holding on to the pilot's seat with her bare hands, even as the plane dipped and bucked.

"Strap in," Dek said. She shoved Gideon's backpack out of the copilot's seat and jerked Tessa down into position. Tessa heard the seat belt click together before she fully understood what was going on.

"What about—Gideon?" Tessa asked.

"That's up to him," Dek said, shrugging. "Seems like he wanted to die before, so . . ."

Tessa was glad to see that Gideon had pulled a rope from somewhere and was tying himself to the column behind the seats. He was still watching the computer screen too.

"No!" he suddenly screamed. "No! The autopilot's putting us down in Shargo!"

"What's Shargo?" Tessa shouted.

Gideon didn't answer her. Now he was yanking the rope back off again, and diving toward the control panel.

"Override!" he screamed. "Override!"

"It won't override now!" Dek screamed back at him.

"What's Shargo?" Tessa yelled again.

Gideon slumped to the floor. He wasn't even trying to protect himself now.

"It's the largest city in the war zone," he said. "There are nine million people there who hate us. And—it's the enemy's military headquarters."

CHAPTER

20

Tessa didn't know what a normal landing was supposed to feel like. But she was pretty sure this wasn't right. The plane rocked violently, side to side. More than once it seemed to be on the verge of completely rolling over. And then when it righted itself, just when Tessa was thinking, *Okay, survived that*, it would jump suddenly, as if hit by a brutal gust of wind.

Dek patted Tessa's hand.

"Sorry!" she yelled, over the noise that sounded like the whole plane was being torn apart. "This old tub wasn't meant to carry passengers. When my bosses retrofitted it for human transport, they weren't exactly trying for comfort, you know?"

She took a close look at Tessa's face, then dug down under the pilot's seat and produced a paper sack.

"Airsickness bag, okay?" Dek said, handing it to Tessa. "Use it if you need to."

Tessa shook her head. She didn't think she was in danger of throwing up. It felt more like her throat had closed over, like she wouldn't even be able to squeeze out the words to ask, *Are we all going to die? Please . . . I don't want to die.*

Gideon leaned over Tessa's seat from behind and yanked the bag from her grasp.

"Give her—another—," he choked out.

And then he was gagging and retching into the bag.

Dek laughed.

"Still think you're so high and mighty, Mr. Military Pilot?" she taunted, even as she reached for another bag for Tessa.

The plane jerked and lurched and rolled. Tessa closed her eyes and bent her head down.

"No, no—*look* at something!" Dek yelled at her. "Watch the movement! It'll fend off the airsickness!"

Tessa wanted to say, *Leave me alone! Let me die in peace!* But just in the short time she'd spent with Dek, she could tell: Dek wouldn't stop bugging her. Dek wasn't the type to ever leave someone in peace.

Tessa opened her eyes and stared at the computer screen. Surprisingly, this did make her stomach feel more settled. But were they supposed to be dropping toward the ground so rapidly?

Gasping and still gagging, Gideon struggled up behind her.

"Trees . . . nothing but trees . . . not supposed to be trees here," he murmured, lunging toward the computer screen again.

Tessa tried to focus on the shapes and colors on the screen, rather than the sensation that the ground was rushing toward them too quickly. The ground did seem to be full of hillocks and mounds of green—she guessed those might be trees.

Gideon dropped the airsickness bag from his face long enough to punch in commands to open a new window down in the corner of the computer screen. Then he called up something recorded—maybe more of the spy satellite video Tessa had seen before. This time Tessa noticed both the geographical coordinates and a date stamped at the bottom of the screen: yesterday's date. Tessa blinked and focused on the scenes: rows and rows of houses and streets and apartment buildings. They looked like they might once have been quite nice, with neatly mowed yards and flowers growing along the sidewalks. But now the yards and flower beds were pitted with craters; facades were ripped from the buildings. In one house lacy curtains fluttered out a window, a portrait of some cozy normalcy Tessa had always longed for. But those curtains, that window, the wall that held it—that was the only part of the house that hadn't been turned into rubble.

Gideon moaned.

"There was a bombing raid here *yesterday morning*," he murmured. "Why aren't *our* cameras showing this? This is all right below us. Why can't we see it from the air?"

He minimized the scenes of destruction, so the trees rushing toward them filled the whole screen.

"Did the enemy just this morning unveil some incredibly advanced masking technology?" he asked. "I've got to tell—"

He reached toward the controls again, but Dek slapped his hands away.

"You are not sending any message out to our military, from this plane, right now," she ordered, in a tone that would have been perfect for a general if it hadn't carried just the slightest hint of little-girl squeakiness. "Are you trying to make our chances of being killed go *over* one hundred percent?"

Gideon paused to retch into his airsickness bag.

"It's just—," he said, when he could speak again.

"Unless the enemy shot down all our spy satellites, our military's seeing the same thing we are," Dek snapped. "Let's focus on doing things that keep us alive, shall we?"

Gideon probably would have kept protesting, but they hit a pocket of air just then that made the whole plane buck wildly. He had one hand on the airsickness bag and one hand stretched out toward the controls—he wasn't holding on to anything solid. He tumbled over backward.

Tessa grabbed for his arm.

She caught his sleeve; he curled his fingers around her wrist.

"Are you trying to pull her arm out of its socket?" Dek shrieked at him. "Do you hurt or kill *everything* you touch?"

Gideon let go.

"No!" Tessa screamed.

But when she looked back, Gideon had only shifted to clutching the back of her seat.

Tessa wouldn't have thought it possible, but the landing got even rougher after that. Maybe the wind currents were more dangerous closer to the Earth's surface; maybe even the autopilot had lost power, and gravity was taking over. The plane shimmied and shook, rolled and throbbed, slammed down toward the ground. This seemed to go on for hours. Tessa's teeth pounded together; her spine jolted against the seat; the belt bit into her hips. And then, even when Tessa was certain they had to be on the ground, they *bounced.*

When they finally stopped moving, Tessa didn't dare to breathe for a full minute.

"Is . . . everyone . . . okay?" she asked in a small voice that sounded tinny and panicked even to her own ears. She had a sudden fear of looking around: What if Dek or Gideon was dead? She kept her eyes focused forward, staring straight at the computer screen, which had gone completely dark.

Suddenly a hand slapped against the screen.

"On! Come! Back! On!"

It was Dek. She'd sprung out of her seat and was alternately hitting the computer screen and slamming her hands against the controls.

"Who designs a computer system to shut down just when you need it most?" she hollered. "Where's the backup power?"

"It . . . serves the . . . military's purposes, not to have a drone plane loaded with all our coding . . . fall into enemy hands," Gideon said in a creaky voice from behind Tessa. He was alive! "So . . . blame your bosses . . . for not . . . retrofitting . . . enough."

Tessa spun around, to see if Gideon looked as pained as he sounded. But the jerky movement was too much for her after the wild landing. Her stomach lurched; her head throbbed; her vision receded and then surged again.

By the time Tessa could see straight once more, Dek had already launched herself from the pilot's seat and was running toward Gideon. He was huddled in a broken-looking way against the padded column.

Okay, Tessa thought. *Dek will take care of him. She's not as heartless as she tries to sound. She's all bark, no bite.*

Dek bent down beside Gideon. But instead of checking for broken bones or dabbing at the cut over his cheek, she immediately began tugging at his shirt.

"We've got to get that uniform off you and hide it!" she cried, her voice brimming with fear. "Tessa, help! If the enemy shows up and sees him wearing that, they'll kill us all!"

Gideon twisted around and shoved her away. She hit the wall hard.

Maybe Gideon wasn't hurt as badly as he looked.

"This uniform may be the only thing that saves us," he insisted. "If I can say, 'I surrender' before they shoot me, they have to treat me like a prisoner of war. There are *rules* for that. Policies they have to follow."

Dek snorted.

"Only way that uniform is going to protect you is if it's bulletproof," she muttered. She rubbed the back of her neck, where she'd hit the wall. "And what's going to protect Tessa and me?"

"I will," Gideon said.

Tessa expected the other two to ask what she thought, to give her a chance to weigh in with her own opinion. Would she have to cast the tie-breaking vote?

But Gideon was already lunging to his feet, already

slamming his hand against the release for the door. The door slid open, and instantly he had his hands raised in the air.

"I surrender!" he screamed out into the open air. Tessa could tell he was trying to make his voice as loud as possible, to reach the ears of snipers who might be hundreds of feet away. "I surrender! I surrender! I . . ."

Gideon stopped talking.

CHAPTER

21

It's amazing what you can notice in a split second. In the instant after Gideon's voice died out, Tessa stared at him so hard that she could see the individual beads of sweat caught in his eyebrows. She could see the crust of a scab already forming over the cut on his cheekbone. She could see the way his hands trembled as he held them in the air. She could see the slight smear of what might be vomit on the formerly pure-white cuff of his uniform sleeve.

But she didn't see any recoil in his body from bullets hitting it; she didn't see any bloom of suddenly gushing blood on the section of the uniform covering his heart.

She kept looking. She seemed incapable of doing anything else.

Not Dek.

"What?" Dek demanded, her voice hoarse with fury or fear. Tessa couldn't be sure which one it was. "You can't just stop like that. You've committed to this course of action—you keep surrendering until they're carrying you away in hand-cuffs and leg irons!"

Gideon turned his head very, very slowly.

"I don't think there's anyone out there," he said in a near whisper. "There's nobody to surrender *to*."

Dek stared at him in disbelief for a moment; then she scrambled toward the door herself and peeked around the edge of it.

Tessa realized that she'd slumped down in the copilot's seat in a way that protected most of her body from the door-way. Only the top of her head and her eyes were exposed.

What do you know, Tessa thought. *Guess I have survival instincts I never knew about.*

But the longer Gideon stood in the open doorway, not being shot, the more foolish Tessa felt for cowering in terror. She even thought Dek looked kind of foolish, clutching the curve of the wall and only barely looking past the strip of rubber that lined the door. Tessa felt like she'd done way too much cowering since she'd stepped onto this plane the night before. She'd done way too much cowering her entire life.

On trembling legs she stood up and went to stand beside Gideon. Standing freely, on her own, she gazed out into enemy territory.

At first glance it looked like Gideon was right: There was no one in sight. There was, actually, very little in sight. Very little except for a vast field of grass, stretching out in all directions.

Or—was this still what you would call grass? In Tessa's experience grass was tufts of muddied green blades that tried to spring up in bare patches of dirt, when people didn't trample it too badly. She'd seen pictures in books of expansive lawns trimmed to almost scientific perfection in the luxurious, prodigal era before the war began. But that had always seemed too fantastical to believe, like gazing at drawings of unicorns or fairies or trolls.

This field did not look like a lawn. For one thing the grass was too tall. Half thinking, *Maybe it's not too smart to just keep standing here, a clear target,* Tessa stepped down into the grass. Much of it reached all the way up to her waist; a few hardy stalks were level with her shoulders. A breeze shuddered across the field, and Tessa almost forgot herself watching the glory of it all, seeing the acres and acres of grass bowing together. It was like music, like a dance. The grass seemed more fully alive than any of the people Tessa had ever known.

"I . . . surrender?" Gideon called again behind her, his voice gone soft and uncertain.

"Would you two idiots stop and think for a second?" Dek hissed from her position still crouched at the edge of the door. "Just because they haven't killed us yet, that doesn't mean nobody's going to."

"So what would you have us do?" Gideon asked mockingly. "Let me guess—you've got some brilliant plan."

"As a matter of fact I do," Dek whispered. "Hasn't it occurred to you yet? For some reason, no one seems to know we're here. Maybe it's *our* military that put some brilliant masking technology on this plane. Maybe it was my bosses.

They'd love it if their planes didn't show up on any radar except their own. And, you know, it's not like they'd tell me about anything like that."

Tessa was surprised to hear a bit of pain throbbing in Dek's voice.

So she resents not being fully trusted, Tessa decided, then pushed the thought to the back of her mind because none of that really mattered right now.

"I don't hear a plan in all that," Gideon complained. "You open your mouth and I just hear, 'Maybe this,' 'Maybe that.' No military ever conquered anybody with maybes."

Tessa thought this must be something his instructors had said a lot at the military academy. He sounded like he was quoting.

"That was background information," Dek said. "Here's the plan: As long as nobody knows we're here, why don't we keep it that way? We sneak away from the plane, find some jet fuel to steal—and some sort of container to steal it in—we come back here, fuel up, and then we're on our merry way. No one gets hurt; we get out of here undetected; everything's good."

Gideon frowned. Tessa could tell he was trying to find something to object to.

"What if someone catches us?" he asked.

"*Then* you surrender," Dek countered. "We can always go back to the original plan if we have to."

Gideon's frown deepened.

"I don't think you can still surrender and be protected under prisoner-of-war laws if you're caught in the middle of a crime," he said. "Like, say, stealing."

Dek threw up her hands.

"Fine! I'll be the one to steal the fuel!" she said. "I'll carry the canister myself. You can stay all pure and innocent and white-uniformed as long as you want!"

Gideon kept glaring at her, but he slid down into the grass beside Tessa. A moment later Dek stepped down alongside them.

Once again, the other two had made a decision without even consulting Tessa.

"Crouch down as you walk," Dek suggested. "No point in being total sitting ducks."

"Shouldn't we try to hide the plane?" Tessa asked.

"Where?" Dek asked.

"How?" Gideon asked. "Even if we could push it somewhere, we'd just leave a trail of crushed grass that would lead right to it."

"Oh," Tessa said, feeling more stupid than ever. She noticed that the blades of grass broke off just as she tiptoed through them. "But we're leaving a trail too!"

"Can't be helped," Dek said with a shrug.

Tessa saw that both of the other two believed they were going to get caught. Maybe they thought it would be better to get caught away from the plane than on it? Or . . . maybe they just thought it was better to try *something* rather than just wait to be killed?

All three of them plodded forward. Tessa wondered if they'd picked a direction on purpose or if it was just a random choice. She wasn't going to embarrass herself further by asking.

Then something jabbed into the side of her shoe.

"Ow!" she cried, reaching down. She came up with a

handful of gravel. "Why would there be rocks in a field of grass?" she asked. She reached down again, and felt around. "There are rocks *everywhere*!" she said. "Rocks, and little bits of broken-up concrete—"

"The enemy's ways are not our ways," Gideon said, and once again it sounded like he was quoting.

Dek reached over and pulled Tessa's hands back.

"It's really better not to touch anything you don't have to touch," Dek said. "I mean, I'm not sure *why* there'd be land mines here, but still . . ."

"Land mines!" Tessa exclaimed, jumping back. She over-reacted, and teetered, almost falling down flat. "You—you think it's possible that there might be land mines here, but you still . . . you just . . ."

She couldn't bring herself to finish the sentence.

Dek shrugged, her ragged, oversized shirt shifting on her scrawny shoulders.

"Well, I have been trying to make sure I step in his footsteps," she said, pointing to Gideon. "It's safer that way."

Gideon turned around. He seemed to be trying to look stoic and brave, but Tessa guessed that he hadn't thought of the possibility of land mines either. When you were used to flying—and not even sitting in the plane—it wasn't something you ever had to think about.

But Gideon just said, "Let's keep moving, all right? The faster we go, the less time we have to spend here, and the less chance someone's going to see us."

He faced forward again and took another step. And another. And another.

Though she had to stretch her legs a ridiculous distance, Dek jumped behind him, landing each time on the same patch of crushed grass Gideon had just left.

She turned around to look at Tessa, who hadn't moved since she'd heard the words "land mines."

"See?" Dek said. "If he doesn't blow up when he steps in that space, we won't blow up either."

Tessa made herself take a step forward. She stopped again.

"It's not fair," she said.

Dek and Gideon both looked at her.

"*Fair*?" Dek repeated. "You flew into enemy territory looking for things to be fair?"

All's fair in love and war, Tessa thought, remembering something she'd read a long time ago. She'd been a little kid and confused; she'd thought that the saying meant that love and war really did make everything fair.

But was that really the issue?

Tessa pushed the thought aside.

"No," she said. "I mean, it's not *right*." Both of the others were staring at her, dumbstruck, but she bumbled on. "We shouldn't just automatically assume that Gideon should be the one in the lead, the one at risk. We should take turns."

"Hey," Dek said. "He's the one who got us into this whole mess. He's the one that flew us into a war zone."

"No," Tessa said again, stubbornly shaking her head. "We each got ourselves into our own mess. I followed him. You stowed away on his plane. We're both responsible for being here too."

These were all such new thoughts for Tessa that it was

amazing she could find the words to explain. There was something about standing in this vast field of grass, something about seeing the wind blow each individual stalk, something about feeling the constant danger—all of that made Tessa see everything differently than she ever had back in Waterford City.

"Tessa," Gideon said gently. "It's all right. I'm military. I was trained for this."

"No," Tessa said. "You weren't. I'm sorry, but all you were ever trained for was to sit at a desk and kill people hundreds of miles away by remote."

Gideon stared at her. Tessa wasn't sure what he saw in her face. Did he see mockery and blame? Did he think she was taunting him as a "fake flyboy" even more cruelly than Dek had? Or did he think she was forgiving him for not being the hero she'd longed to idolize?

Tessa wasn't sure what showed in her face, because she wasn't sure which thing she believed—or which she believed most strongly. All she knew was that she couldn't walk the entire way across the field with Gideon taking all the risk.

"Okay," Dek said. "It's official. You've both got martyr complexes. You two want to take turns leading the way, fine. But let's *keep moving*. You can trade off every twenty paces. And, here." She scooped up a handful of gravel and dropped it into Tessa's hands. "Whoever's in the lead, you test the route you're going to take by throwing rocks at it first."

Tessa expected Gideon to protest—either to refuse to let Tessa ever take the lead, or to insist to Dek that she take an equal turn at the front too. But Gideon just squinted at Tessa for a long moment, as if seeing her for the first time. Then he pointed off into the distance.

"That's where we're headed," he said.

Tessa stood on her tiptoes, making herself nearly as tall as Gideon. Now she could see past the rippling grass, to a structure that barely topped the horizon. It could have been an excessively tall tree, an odd sight in the midst of all the grass.

Or—it could have been something man-made.

"I think that's an old air-control tower," Gideon said. "I saw it on our way down. It looks abandoned, don't you think? We get up there, we'll be able to see for miles."

Tessa could tell he was being very careful not to add a depressing corollary: *Or, if there's someone up there, they're going to be able to see us a long, long time before we see them.*

CHAPTER

22

It was slow going. Every few steps the person in the lead had to throw out a handful of gravel, walk forward, then scoop up another handful to throw. It amazed Tessa that there was always more gravel around to throw. This seemed man-made too, or at least of human design. Nothing in nature would dump tons of gravel in a field of grass, would it?

Once they got close enough to the tower to see the windows at the top, they slowed down even more, stopping every few steps to watch for movement, to listen for the first hint of any shouted commands. Gideon began walking with his hands high in the air, back in the pose of a surrendering soldier. He walked that way for so long that Tessa was certain his arms must have gone numb, but he didn't complain.

While Gideon was busy constantly surrendering, Tessa

took over the job of throwing out the handfuls of gravel to test the route ahead for him.

Tessa remembered the question Dek had asked her back on the plane, as soon as Gideon was out of earshot: *He your boyfriend?* She remembered the way Gideon's mother had looked at her, as Tessa had walked into Gideon's bedroom. She remembered the taunt nasty Cordina Kurdle from school had flung at her back at the auditorium the day of the ruined award ceremony: *If you and the hero are so close, why aren't you running after him?*

All that had made Tessa feel a little bit sleazy. She had run after Gideon. She had chased after him all the way into enemy territory. In her wildest dreams she might have hoped for a hug or a kiss from the glowing hero.

She never could have imagined how intimate she could feel, not even touching him but walking together in silence through a field of grass, throwing rocks out in front of him, trying to keep him alive.

Was it because I spoke up, and volunteered to risk my life too? Did that make us true partners?

Something moved at the top of the tower. In a flash Dek had her arm reared back and began throwing rocks toward the dark windows.

"Stop! Stop!" Gideon begged. "It doesn't work for me to surrender if you're launching projectiles at them! They'll retaliate!"

A flurry of wings flapped out the tower windows.

"Guys, look! Stop arguing! Stop throwing things! It's only birds!" Tessa cried, pulling back on Dek's arm.

Dek dropped the rest of her handful of gravel and wiped her hand across her sweaty forehead, leaving a trail of dirt.

"Yeah, and we wouldn't have known that if I hadn't flushed them out," she bragged.

Tessa looked at Dek carefully. Dek had been the cautious one before. Why was she taking risks now?

"You already knew it was just birds, didn't you?" Tessa asked. "How were you so sure?"

Dek shrugged.

"Educated guess," she said. "Look at all the bird droppings coming down from those windows. I bet they're even thicker inside. Nobody's going to be hanging out in the midst of all that. Or—if they are—it's not going to be somebody who'd know or respect the rules about how to treat a surrendering enemy soldier. So I *had* to go on the offensive."

Tessa squinted up toward the top of the tower. Now that Dek had pointed it out, Tessa noticed the streaks of white and gray and brown running down from the windows. And Tessa could see now that all the windows were broken. Only a few jagged shards of glass remained in place, throwing off reflected light from the sun.

She looked to Gideon, wondering what brilliant deductions he'd figured out, staring at the tower.

"Still," Gideon said stubbornly. He wasn't looking at the tower. He was glaring at Dek. "Still. We have to make it look like we've come in peace."

"But we haven't," Dek said. "We can't. Not when our whole country's at war."

There didn't seem to be anything to say to that. They

walked on, each step tense and fearful. It was a relief finally to reach the base of the tower, out of sight of the dark windows overhead. Tessa saw that a metal door hung open, rusted half off its hinges, revealing a flight of stairs inside.

"So we're going to be really, really quiet climbing up there?" Tessa whispered. "Just in case?"

"Won't work," Gideon said, shaking his head. "We don't have any weapons with us. If someone up there does . . ." He leaned his head into the stairwell, tilted it upward and shouted, "We surrender! We surrender!"

The words echoed back at him, -ender . . . -ender . . . -ender . . . But no other voice replied.

Gideon pulled his head back out into the sunlight.

"You two want to wait here while I go up?" he asked.

Yes, Tessa thought. But somehow it seemed like it would be more frightening to stand around at the bottom of the tower, waiting.

"I'll go with you," she said.

She turned toward Dek, expecting the other girl to say, Okay! Let me know what you find up there! But Dek was already headed for the stairs.

"I'm in," she said.

Why? Tessa wondered. Why isn't she letting Gideon and me take all the risk, like she did before?

Tessa noticed the stiff way Dek held her shoulders, the way she clenched her jaw as she walked.

Oh, Tessa thought. Dek doesn't trust us. She isn't sure we'd tell her the truth about what we'd see.

All three of them began climbing the stairs together. Tessa

guessed that Dek wasn't worried about any land mines being left here, because she wasn't making any effort to walk behind the other two.

Birds fluttered around them, darting for the open door.

Oh, yeah, Tessa thought. *If there were any explosives around here, the birds would have set them off already.*

She was proud of herself for figuring this out. She turned and looked behind her, and realized that she, Dek, and Gideon were leaving footprints in the thick layer of bird droppings.

And that's another reason for Dek to be convinced there's no one above us in this tower. Anyone else would have left footprints too.

This helped Tessa relax a little climbing the stairs. But it still wasn't a pleasant experience. The bird droppings covered the stair railings too, so Tessa didn't want to hold on, even in spots where the concrete of the stairs had crumbled away. The farther they climbed, the darker it got, since there were no windows actually in the stairwell. Two flights up, Gideon pulled a flashlight out of somewhere—and muttered, almost apologetically, "Standard military issue." That helped a little. The three of them just had to cluster together, staying near the light.

Finally, panting and sweating, they reached the end of the stairs. Another door sagged from its hinges here, more rust than anything else, and Gideon shoved gingerly past it, into a wide open room.

"We surrender?" he said softly, but this was clearly pointless. The room held nothing but broken glass and twisted metal and the thickest layer of bird droppings Tessa had ever seen. With a complaining cry, one last crow swooped out the broken window.

Tessa startled at the noise, then bent over, her hands on her knees, and tried to catch her breath.

"What . . . a relief," she murmured, her heart still pumping hard, but only from the exertion and the surprise of the crow. "We're safe after all."

Gideon didn't pause even to take a breath. He strode directly to the window. He stared out it, horror spreading across his face.

"No, no, no!" he screamed. He pounded his fist against the concrete wall. "There can't be this many lies!"

CHAPTER

23

Tessa rushed over to see what he was screaming about.

The field of grass lay peacefully before them. Off in the distance she thought she could make out the round hump of the top of their airplane, but it looked totally undisturbed. Far beyond that there were woods, and, even beyond that, a glimmer of water.

Tessa saw nothing that was the least bit upsetting.

"What's your problem?" Dek asked, in the exasperated tone that people used with tantrum-throwing toddlers.

"It's all wrong!" Gideon exclaimed, shaking his arms for emphasis—his hands-in-the-air surrender pose transformed from showing meekness to signaling fury. "Everything in sight! I *know* where we are! This should be the main air-traffic control tower for the largest military air base in Shargo. Out there"—he gestured wildly toward the field of grass—"there should be dozens and dozens of runways. One huge square of concrete after another. And over there"—he pointed at the woods—"that should be on-base housing for hundreds of pilots. And beyond that"—he gestured more broadly, indicating a farther distance—"we should be able to see skyscrapers. Skyscrapers! Do either of you see any skyscrapers?"

"No, but . . . don't you think that means you're probably . . . confused?" Tessa asked hesitantly.

"I'm not confused! Something's really, really wrong here!" Gideon screamed back at her.

A bird starting to fly in the window saw his waving arms and flew back out.

"Keep your voice down," Dek hissed at him. "And—tell us why we should believe you and not believe what we see with our own eyes."

Gideon pointed toward the curve of water near the horizon.

"That's Lake Mish," he said. "And over there—see that line of blue leading to the lake?—that's the Shargo River. I *know* this landscape. That's exactly how Lake Mish and the Shargo River *are*. I've looked at this area a million times on spy satellite footage. I've done hundreds of simulation attack plans flying over it. I've done simulations dropping bombs on this very tower!"

"Simulations," Dek said. "Not real."

Gideon glared at her.

"In simulations," he said, "everything is as real as they can make it, without actually having the planes in the air."

Tessa was staring out at the field of grass, thinking about

THE ALWAYS WAR •

the weird way the gravel was scattered all over it. She gasped.

"What would happen," she said, "if people just abandoned a bunch of runways? Or—any area where there's a lot of concrete? After a while wouldn't it crack? Wouldn't grass start growing up in the cracks?" She could remember seeing this back home in Waterford City, the way untended parking lots always sprouted weeds. "And then, wouldn't the roots of the grass start breaking up the concrete? Until . . . eventually . . . it's nothing but gravel?"

"You think the enemy would abandon their biggest airfield?" Gideon asked incredulously. "You think they'd abandon *Shargo*? Why?"

"Hey," Dek said, "maybe our side's really winning. Maybe we've already won."

Tessa thought about everything they'd seen flying over enemy territory.

"Maybe they just show you old footage for simulations," she said. "Just for your practice. Remember back on the plane, when you were getting all upset about seeing nothing but trees? There was one spot where I thought I saw something brick alongside one of the trees—like an old chimney, maybe?"

"There was a bombing raid there *yesterday morning*," Gideon reminded her. "A tree can't grow out of a chimney in one day!"

"Yeah, and according to the computer, there was a bombing raid right on top of us *this* morning down by Santl," Tessa countered. "Sometimes computers can be wrong."

Gideon sagged against the wall. Tessa didn't want to think

about how much of the bird droppings were rubbing off on his white uniform.

"I wasn't going to tell you this," he said in a hoarse voice. "Remember that video I showed you of the people dying in *my* bombing raid, in the battle I fought in?"

"Yes," Tessa said, very gently, because somehow that seemed like the right way to speak to Gideon right now.

"Well, I was never supposed to see that. We pilots don't have that kind of security clearance," he said. "I had to hack my way in."

"Huh," Dek grunted. "And here I had you pegged as a total straight-arrow military type. Not *that* much of a rule-breaker. Definitely not a hacker."

Gideon didn't even glance her way.

"I had to see what I'd done," he said pleadingly. "What I'd caused. What I was responsible for."

"Okay," Tessa said soothingly. "But—"

"So that's proof, you know?" Gideon said. "What we saw of my raid, of the raid here in Shargo—that's what the *generals* see! It's real! It's not some made-up simulation for fake pilots!"

He hit the wall again and twisted his head about even more crazily, his face going even more wild-eyed. He flinched just at the sight of the peaceful grass, the peaceful trees. He looked like he might do anything—jump out the window or attack Tessa and Dek or just collapse in a heap of huge, soul-racking sobs.

"Calm down," Dek said. She took a step toward him, her hands up in the air in a gesture that was clearly supposed to show that she, at least, was no threat. It was the same way someone might approach a dangerous animal.

"What do you know about any of this?" Gideon asked bitterly.

"Nothing," Dek admitted. She took another step closer. "But I'm sure there's some explanation, something we haven't thought of because we don't have enough information. You know that's how the military works. The people at the top only tell the people at the bottom certain things, just enough to get them to do what they want."

Tessa expected Gideon to argue with this. If nothing else, she wanted him to say, *I wasn't someone at the bottom! I'm the hero!* But he only shrugged, probably grinding more of the bird droppings into his white uniform.

"That's how the black market rings work too," Dek admitted. "Sometimes, if you're sneaky enough, you can find out things people don't want you to know." She flashed him a grin. "But you already know that, if you were hacking into top-secret video."

Gideon didn't answer. Dek kept inching toward him.

"The thing is, other times you just have to make do," she said. "All you can do is pick a course of action based on what you do know, what seems most likely to keep you alive." She reached Gideon's side and put a steadying hand on his arm. She tugged him gently around to face the window once again. "This is one of those times. Do you see anything out there that looks like a jet-fuel tank?"

Gideon raised a shaking hand and pointed to the right, to a place where the grass was short and stubby rather than long and flowing.

"In all the simulations," he said dully, "the fuel tanks were underground, right about there. We . . . we got bonus points if we dropped the bombs in a way that cracked the concrete, made the tanks explode. I did that once. That's how I got promoted, how I qualified to go on real bombing raids."

Dek started to pull him back away from the window, but he locked his muscles in place. He kept staring out at the peaceful grass with a haunted look on his face, as if his eyes were showing him an entirely different scene.

"That's how I qualified to kill people," he said.

Dek patted his arm.

"Okay," she said. "It's okay. All that's over now."

Gideon turned and looked at her as if she'd just told him the biggest lie of all.

24

The fuel tanks were still there.

Tessa might have expected Gideon to gloat, to tell Dek, *See, I am not making all of this up! I do know what I'm talking about!* But he just stood there in silence, a vacant expression on his face, while Dek muttered on and on about how hard it was going to be getting any fuel out when all the pumping mechanisms had rusted and rotted away, and, "Even if we manage to draw some of that fuel up to the surface, how are we going to carry it over to the plane? And what if it's too contaminated to be any good?"

Tessa didn't even pretend to understand the strategies Dek came up with. Dek ordered both Tessa and Gideon around like slaves. She had them take apart pieces of the plane's engine to carry over to the fuel tanks to reassemble into a makeshift contraption for siphoning up the fuel. Curved pieces of metal from the plane's wings became the carrying jugs to take the fuel back to the plane, one shallow, easily spilled load at a time. Tessa alone must have made thirty trips back and forth.

Even after just a few trips Tessa's feet ached, her back ached, her arms ached. She got a nasty cut on her leg from the metal, and it burned when her own sweat ran down into it. Her throat burned too, because it turned out that there wasn't enough water on the airplane, and Dek insisted on rationing it out in small sips.

Even Tessa's fingernails hurt, because she still had to scoop up gravel to test out a safe path without any land mines between the plane and the fuel tanks.

Don't think, Tessa told herself. *Just walk.*

And then that bothered her, because wasn't that pretty much how people did things back in Waterford City?

She thought about Dek's explanation of how the military worked, how black market rings worked: *The people at the top only tell the people at the bottom certain things, just enough to get them to do what they want.*

As far as Tessa could tell, that was how the whole world worked. And she was so far down at the bottom that nobody had ever bothered to tell her anything except "Do this," "Do that," "Scrub this," "Carry that."

And she'd always gone along with it, until she'd met Gideon.

I was capable of figuring out that the gravel in the grass is the remains of all those military runways Gideon saw in his simulations, Tessa told herself. *Why aren't I thinking as hard as I can, trying to figure out all the other mysteries we've encountered today?*

Tessa's brain started hurting too, aching just as violently as her back and her feet and her arms.

She decided to start with just one small bit of the whole puzzle:

Dek.

"How'd you get to know so much about airplanes and flying and fuel pumps and everything?" Tessa asked Dek on her next trip to the fuel tanks.

Dek balanced a piece of rubber hose that had come out of the plane engine at the edge of the curved metal Tessa was using to haul the fuel. She undid some sort of clamp she'd rigged up, and a thin stream of rusty liquid trickled out.

"My dad was a mechanic," Dek said. "Even when I was a baby, he'd hand me motors and stuff like that to play with. So I was either going to die from choking on a bolt or a nut or a washer, or I was going to grow up knowing my way around engines. I guess it could have gone either way."

The fuel was flowing so slowly it hadn't reached anywhere near the rim of the metal piece. Tessa thought there was time for another question.

"So wasn't your dad really proud when you were chosen for the military academy?" she asked.

Dek became very still.

"He was dead by then," she said. "Both my parents were."

"Yeah, but you could have honored him by joining up," Tessa argued. "You could have dedicated everything you did in the military to his memory."

Dek shut down the clamp on the hose.

"You don't know what you're talking about," she said in a voice that was like a door slamming in Tessa's face.

Tessa's legs started shaking.

You're a little kid, she wanted to tell Dek. *You're just a street brat. Working for criminals. Who are you to go around acting like you're better than me? You're no better than a flea. A gnat. A—*

Tessa remembered that those were the same taunts that nasty Cordina Kurdle had flung at Tessa, back at Gideon's awards ceremony. Was this what it felt like to be Cordina, to feel so worthless that you had to tear everyone else down too?

Tessa blinked back tears. She was hungry, she was thirsty, she was tired, she hurt—and she still thought there was a decent chance she and Dek and Gideon were going to get killed. Why did even talking to Dek have to be painful?

What in life wasn't pain?

Gideon came up behind them just then, back from his own fuel-carrying trip to the plane.

"I think we should finish up, make this our last trip," he said, casting an anxious glance toward the sky. "That fuel gauge says we've got half a tank now, and that's more than enough to get us back across the border into Eastam."

Tessa could tell he was worried about having to spend even a second longer here on the ground, exposed, in enemy territory.

"How long you think we're going to need to stay in the air once we're across the border?" Dek asked.

The glance that passed between her and Gideon was charged with an unusual undercurrent, some sort of understanding that excluded Tessa.

This made Tessa even madder.

I am not going to keep being the stupid person here, she thought. *I can at least try to figure this out. Fuel . . . the border . . .*

Then she understood.

"You think our own border guards are going to shoot us down," she said.

Gideon wouldn't look her in the eye.

"They're trained to make split-second decisions," he said. "We'll be coming from enemy territory, we won't be tagged in their system as one of their own returning from a legitimate bombing raid—"

"So hack into their system again and change that!" Tessa suggested.

Gideon shook his head.

"No way I could do that from enemy territory," he said.

"But—our plane still has defensive shields, right?" Tessa asked.

"Not that work against our own missiles," Gideon said miserably. "See, everything's coded . . ."

Tessa felt dizzy, unable to take all this in. *Then . . . if it's not safe to fly across the border, let's just stay here,* she almost said. But they'd already run out of water, and Tessa didn't think they had any more of the nutri-squares. And, anyway, they were in enemy territory. Even if the area around them seemed deserted, every moment they spent here was borrowed time.

"I would think . . . if it's dangerous to cross the border . . . we'd want to have as much fuel in our tank as possible," she said, still grasping for something hopeful to say. "So we can fly all along the border, until we find the safest place to cross."

"As soon as we can see the guards, they can see us," Gideon said lifelessly.

"And the more fuel we have, the more likely it is that our plane will explode when we get hit," Dek added.

Tessa slumped, almost spilling the precious, dangerous fuel pooled on her piece of metal. Wasn't there any possibility to hold on to, any reason for hope?

"We have parachutes," Gideon offered.

Tessa thought she finally saw the full picture, with all the depressing details Gideon and Dek had agreed upon in a single glance. Gideon and Dek were almost certain they were going to get shot down. All they could hope for was that they could make it out of the crash alive.

And land on the proper side of the border.

Nobody spoke as they carried the last load of fuel back to the plane, along with the various pieces of plane parts that had been made over into a fuel siphon and were soon to be returned to their original purpose. Dek and Gideon worked together to reassemble the plane; Tessa stood nearby handing them screws and bolts and tools. Most of the time she gave them the wrong thing at the wrong time, but neither of them complained.

Another question started growing in Tessa's mind, but she held off asking it until everything was back in order on the plane.

"How did we manage to fly across the border without being shot down in the first place?" she asked, as she climbed back in the door. "When we flew into enemy territory, I mean?"

"The guards were only watching out for the other direction," Gideon said. "And—I guess we got lucky."

"We'll get lucky again," Tessa said. "We will."

Neither Gideon nor Dek answered her.

They took off into a clear blue sky so achingly beautiful that Tessa wished they could just keep going up and up and up forever. But they had to level off; they had to turn toward the east.

Down below, Lake Mish sparkled in the late-afternoon sunlight. There was a flash of land, green and seemingly untouched, and then the water came back into sight.

"Lake Mish goes on *this far*?" Tessa gasped.

"No, that's another lake," Gideon said. "There are five of them: Mish, Perry Ore, Ree, Terry O, and You're Wrong."

"'You're Wrong'?" Tessa repeated. "Somebody named a lake You're Wrong?"

"I think it might have had a different name a long time ago, before the war," Gideon said. "But, you know, this is what we're fighting over. The water. So this tradition started, whenever one side took the lake back from the other, they'd taunt, 'You're wrong. You're wrong.' The name stuck."

"Back and forth," Dek muttered, adjusting her seat belt. "Back and forth."

Tessa just gaped at both of them. It had never occurred to her that there might be a reason behind the war, something the two sides were actually fighting over. The war just was.

"We're fighting over *water*?" she asked weakly.

Gideon nodded, his eyes focused on the computer screen.

"Yeah. Westam ran out of water. Eastam still had a lot," he

said. "So Westam attacked. And the war's been going on ever since."

"*I* heard the lakes and rivers in the war zone are probably all so contaminated now that they're no good to anyone," Dek murmured. "It's crazy!"

Tessa sat back in her seat.

"Why didn't I know this?" she asked. "Why don't they teach this in school? Why am I so stupid?"

Dek glanced at her.

"Well, your school's probably designed to make you stupid. Most of them are set up that way. They don't want people asking questions," she said.

"Sorry *I* wasn't smart enough to qualify for the military academy," Tessa muttered.

"Really . . . the military academy's no better," Gideon said, pacing behind her. "They didn't want us asking questions there, either. They just wanted us following orders."

His pacing was making Tessa nervous. She was already nervous enough.

"Aren't you going to tie yourself to the column again when we get close to the border?" she asked.

"No," Gideon said. "I need to be free to jump out the door if I have to."

Tessa saw that he'd already strapped a parachute on his back.

"You and I have eject buttons on our seats," Dek explained. "You hear anything hitting our plane, anything at all, you hit that button immediately. You and your seat will shoot up in the air and then the parachute will come out of your seat cushion."

Tessa wondered if she'd be able to do that when the time

came. She'd never been good with her hands. Under pressure she'd probably hit the right side of her seat when the button was on the left, or the left side when it was on the right or— which side was it on again?

She looked down. The button glowed red on her right armrest, under a plastic cover that she'd have to slide back and out of the way.

"We should be able to see the border in five minutes," Gideon announced behind her. "Four minutes thirty seconds. Four minutes . . ."

Tessa tensed, straining her eyes to see far into the distance on the computer screen. Then she looked back at the eject button, reassuring herself that it was still there.

I don't want to die echoed in her head. *I don't want to die.*

The words were still urgent, but there was something calmer now about her silent pleas. She'd had that moment of communion with Gideon, taking turns with him in danger. She hadn't felt like his equal, exactly, but she'd felt . . . worthy. And she'd seen the grass waving in the wind; she'd seen lakes like glass gleaming in the sun.

Who was she kidding? None of that made her feel ready to die. It made her want to live *more.*

"Three minutes to the border," Gideon continued with his countdown. "Two minutes thirty seconds . . ."

Tessa went back to straining her eyes staring at the computer screen. Trees . . . trees . . . no planes yet . . . no missiles either . . .

"What?" Gideon said. "How could they have changed the boundaries of the border *today?*"

Tessa wanted to ask him if he thought they'd moved the border closer or farther away. But there was no time. Because the plane swerved suddenly, almost as if a giant hand had grabbed it and jerked it off its regular path.

Out of the corner of her eye Tessa saw Dek sliding back the plastic cover from her armrest and plunging her finger toward the red button beneath.

"Tessa, now! Eject!" Dek screamed. "Gideon! The door!"

Tessa fumbled, her hands clumsy and shaking. She had to use both hands to slide the plastic cover back; her finger slipped off the button the first time she tried to hit it. But she tried again, slamming the eject button down as hard as she possibly could.

Nothing happened.

25

Tessa thought she'd done something wrong—*Of course I'd mess up this, too*, she thought. *Can't even press a button properly.*

But then she noticed that Dek's seat hadn't budged either. Dek was hitting the eject button on her armrest again and again and again, and screaming out, "Come on! Come on! Eject!"

And Gideon was over by the door, pounding on the latch there just as doggedly—and failing just as completely.

"Alert!" a mechanical-sounding voice called from the computer. "You are hereby put on notice that all control of this plane has been transferred to the Eastam military. No system will function without our permission."

Dek kept pounding on her eject button.

Gideon slumped against the wall.

"It's no use," he said in a dead voice. "They're not going to let us escape."

"Then—we hide!" Dek exclaimed. "Come on, Tessa! Into the closet!"

She already had her seat belt off and was halfway out of her chair when the mechanical voice sounded again.

"Lieutenant-Pilot Thrall!" the voice boomed. "Please confirm presence of two civilian passengers—Tessa Stilfin and Dekaterina Pratel. Is that correct?"

"Dekaterina?" Tessa repeated numbly. "Who's . . . Oh—*Dek*?"

She stared at Dek's spiky hair and ragged, oversized clothes, which were now filthy as well after all Dek's work on the plane engine and with the fuel tanks. Applying the fancy name Dekaterina to Dek seemed so much like a mistake that Tessa almost forgot that her own name had been called out, too.

"Shh," Dek whispered to Tessa. Then she turned to Gideon and commanded, "Lie."

Gideon gave a minimal shrug, barely bothering to move his shoulders up and down.

"They already know," he said. "They've got cameras. Out there." He pointed toward the windows. "They can see in well enough to identify all of us. You think it's going to matter if I tell the truth or a lie? They can hear us too." He looked at the computer screen and muttered, "Yes. Presence of two civilians confirmed."

Dek remained half up and half down, as if considering all of this.

"Please resume all seat belt usage," the mechanical voice said. "Dekaterina Pratel, please return to your seat."

Dek sat, a stunned look on her face.

"There are only two seat belts and three people," Tessa said. "What are you going to do about that?"

Stupid, stupid, stupid, she told herself. Why try to antagonize the military when even Dek was taking a sit-down-and-shut-up approach?

Because Gideon isn't going to take care of himself, she thought. *So someone else has to.*

"Lieutenant-Pilot Thrall, you are instructed to tie yourself to the center column," the mechanical voice said. "That is an order."

Without a word Gideon pulled the parachute from his back and refashioned the straps into a makeshift belt, lashing himself to the center column.

Nobody spoke as the plane sped on.

They can see us. They can hear us. What good would talking do? Tessa wondered.

Still, she started trying to catch the gaze of Dek or Gideon, hoping one of them could convey in a glance, *We're going to be all right; I've got everything figured out,* or *I'll watch out for you,* or even just, *At least we're still alive; at least we're in this together.* But Gideon had his eyes closed. And Dek was staring intently at the computer screen and the instrument panel, observing every change in altitude and velocity. Several times she even reached out for the controls, drawing back her hand only when the controls jerked themselves out of her grasp.

After the fifth or sixth time Dek tried this—proving yet again that she couldn't change anything—the plane began to angle gently downward all by itself.

"We're going to land?" Dek murmured. "Where?"

Behind her, tied to the column, Gideon answered without opening his eyes.

"Headquarters," he said. "Military headquarters."

"What will they do to us?" Tessa asked, and she was ashamed that her voice came out in a panicky squeak.

Gideon just shook his head. Dek went back to staring.

The plane began to drop out of the sky so rapidly that Tessa had to tell herself, *They wouldn't crash us into the ground on purpose. If nothing else, they wouldn't want to damage the plane. Would they?*

"And I thought the autopilot emergency landing was rough!" Dek murmured. She raised her voice. "Hello, out there! Don't you know you have to land planes differently with people on board?"

The plane seemed to hover in the air for a long moment before angling downward again. Now Tessa felt like a feather floating gently on a breeze.

"Thank you," Dek muttered.

Gideon stayed silent, his face as pale and sweaty as when he'd run from receiving the medal of honor.

And then, before Tessa knew it, they were on the ground. The plane pulled up to a stop and the engine clicked off. The door sprang open.

Dek was looking back at Gideon.

"I always think there's more dignity in walking out to meet

your fate under your own power, rather than being dragged off in chains," she said. "Don't you?"

For a moment Tessa thought Gideon hadn't even heard Dek. But then he leaned forward and began doggedly picking at the knots in the rope tied around him.

Tessa eased her own seat belt off. She felt antsy and tense. What happened to people who stole airplanes from the military? What happened to people who sneaked out into enemy territory—and then came back?

Tessa didn't have the slightest idea, because she'd never heard of anybody doing such a thing. Should she beg and plead and say, *Look, I never meant to do anything wrong. I didn't know where we were going. I didn't know the plane was stolen?*

Or would that just make Gideon and Dek look guiltier?

Two men and two women in light blue uniforms stepped up to the door of the airplane.

"We will escort you to the general's office," one of the men said.

Tessa saw the contrast between their cheap-looking uniforms and the heavy, stiff cloth of Gideon's uniform. She decided that these four were low-level flunkies, not anyone who would be making decisions. She tried to read in their faces some hint of what they thought was going to happen to her and Gideon and Dek, but their expressions were blank.

They probably don't know any more than I do, Tessa thought.

Gideon finished untying his knots and silently turned to follow one of the men. Dek and then Tessa trailed after him. The uniformed women walked on either side of them, and the other man walked behind them.

Like a walking cage, Tessa thought.

She couldn't see any sign that the four escorts were carrying weapons, but that didn't mean that they weren't. Anyway, she was sure that the hallway they stepped into had cameras and listening devices. If the military had been able to see and hear what Tessa, Gideon, and Dek were doing on the airplane, they could certainly see and hear everything in their own headquarters.

The hall led into another hall, and then another one. Tessa gave up trying to keep track of the pattern of intersections and corners and curves. Maybe Gideon and Dek were able to do that; maybe they were just as lost as she was. The halls seemed designed as a maze intended to confuse any outsiders. At one point Tessa was almost certain they'd turned to the right three times, possibly even bringing them back to the section they'd been in before. But maybe it just seemed that way because all the halls looked alike, gray and utilitarian.

And then the hallways started looking nicer, with carpet on the floor and lighter and lighter gray paint. The plaques on the doors they passed were fancier.

After a long stretch of no turns, the man leading the way turned to the right. Gideon froze, and Tessa and Dek almost ran into him.

"What?" Gideon asked. "General Walsh's office is that way."

He pointed straight ahead. So he had been keeping track; he did know where they were.

The blue-uniformed escorts looked impassively at him.

"We're not taking you to General Walsh," the man in the

front said, barely bothering to turn around. "Our orders are to take you to General Kantoff."

"But—General Kantoff is in charge of the entire military! He's the head commander!" Gideon protested. "This—this is just a pilots' issue . . ."

"We have our orders," the man in the front said. He kept walking.

Gideon stumbled going around the corner, and Dek and Tessa both reached out to catch him. He shook off their hands.

"I'm fine," he mumbled. "I—"

He looked wild-eyed and desperate again, as if he might do anything.

"Careful," Dek whispered. "Our lives are on the line here too."

Did she think they were all going to be executed? Was that the punishment for stealing a military plane and flying it into enemy territory?

Whatever Dek thought, her words had an impact on Gideon. He straightened up, his posture changing into an exact copy of the escort's in front of him. He started walking again.

When Gideon caught up with the lead escort, he leaned forward and told the man, "Dek and Tessa didn't have anything to do with entering enemy airspace. Let them go."

The lead escort kept his head facing forward. He didn't break his stride.

"That would violate orders," he said. "We have to follow orders."

They reached the end of the hall. Here there was only one

door in an entire expanse of wall. The door was solid wood, stretching from the floor to the ceiling, bigger and more impressive than any other door they'd passed before.

Tessa felt smaller and more insignificant than ever. She wanted to shrink down and hide behind Gideon. No—she wanted to shrink down and disappear completely, perhaps between two strands of carpet fiber. But she noticed a curious thing: Gideon, the four blue-uniformed escorts, and even Dek all stood taller approaching the imposing door, as if their instincts told them to puff up their chests and try to look bigger.

Even more proof that they belong in the military and I don't, Tessa thought.

She expected someone to knock at the door or just open it, but apparently that wasn't the protocol. Everyone just stood there, in formation, waiting.

"Yes?" A disembodied voice floated out from a speaker beside the door.

"Officer McKutcheon, Squad D, reporting as ordered, with Lieutenant-Pilot Gideon Thrall and two civilians," the lead escort said, saluting the door.

There must be cameras, Tessa thought. *Someone's watching every bit of this.*

She resisted the urge to crane her neck and look around to locate all the cameras and listening devices in the hallway. They were probably too well hidden for her to find, anyway.

And then she forgot about all that, because the door began to swing open.

"Squad D, dismissed!" the voice barked from the speaker.

For the first time the escorts seemed to falter. They exchanged puzzled glances.

"But don't we have to actually walk with the subjects into your—," the lead escort began.

"I said, dismissed!" the voice barked again.

The escorts, in unison, made an about-face and all but marched away.

So . . . should we try to run away? Since no one's guarding us now? Tessa wondered. *Maybe if we did something to disable the cameras—wherever they are . . .*

She tried to catch Gideon's or Dek's gaze, tried to signal that the three of them could make some plan, work together.

But Gideon and Dek were already stepping forward, entering the doorway.

They're smarter than me, Tessa thought. *They know what's possible and what isn't.*

She gulped and stepped through the doorway after them.

CHAPTER

26

The office they entered was luxurious. The first thing Tessa saw was an entire wall taken up with plaques and photos, all very tastefully displayed. Walking past, she saw that the metal on the plaques appeared to be solid gold; the photos were of presidents and generals and other famous people that even she recognized.

Below her feet the carpet was thick and soft. It led up to an imposing desk in the center of a cluster of heavy leather chairs.

A man with perfect posture sat behind the desk. He looked like he might be older than Tessa's parents—maybe fifty, maybe even sixty. But in Tessa's experience fifty- and sixty-year-olds looked flabby and sloppy and defeated, their eyes hazy with alcohol or drugs or despair. This man's green eyes were sharp and clear and seemed to see even what Tessa and Gideon and Dek were thinking. He had salt-and-pepper hair, cropped so precisely that Tessa suspected he got it cut whenever it grew more than a millimeter too long. And his white uniform looked even more pristine than Gideon's had, back in the Waterford City auditorium. The collar alone was starched and ironed to such an exact edge that it probably could be used as a weapon.

"Sit," the man said, nodding toward the leather chairs in front of his desk.

Tessa wanted to object—she and Gideon and Dek were all covered in grease and dirt and sweat. None of them belonged on fancy leather. But Gideon and Dek sat down without saying anything, so Tessa followed suit.

The man—General Kantoff, Tessa realized—leaned forward and lifted a lid from a glass jar at the edge of his desk.

"Cigar?" he asked Gideon.

Gideon looked at the general.

"You offered me a cigar the last time I was in your office, after I killed all those people," Gideon said, in a voice that he seemed to be struggling to control. "I haven't killed anyone this time. I violated the military code, sections 45, 832, and 368. But I didn't kill anyone."

The general watched Gideon for a moment. Then he put the lid back on the glass jar.

"I'll take that as a no," the general said.

He sat back in his chair.

Gideon had his head down, waiting. When nobody said anything, he looked up again.

"Didn't you hear me?" Gideon asked. "I violated three sections of the military code! I just confessed! Any one of those should be grounds for a court-martial!"

"I am aware," the general said dryly, "of your indiscretions."

"Indiscretions?" Gideon asked. "Those are crimes! Crimes that I alone committed—they had nothing to do with it!"

He waved his arm wildly toward Tessa and Dek, seated on either side of him.

"Well, that's settled," Dek said. "How about if Tessa and I just show ourselves out?"

Nobody answered her, and she made no move to leave. Tessa thought, *Guess we should take that as a no too.*

The general had his eyes fixed on Gideon.

"Lieutenant-Pilot Thrall is a very sick young man," the general said speculatively.

"Sick?" Tessa echoed in surprise. "I thought he was supposed to be a hero! That's what everyone said—that's what the military said!"

It startled her to hear her own voice. After everything that had happened, everything she'd found out, everything she'd witnessed with her own eyes and ears—did she still think she could believe in Gideon as a hero? If the general intoned in his most solemn voice, *Yes, yes, Gideon is a hero*, would she automatically agree? Would she think that whatever he said was right just because he was the one saying it?

The general didn't say that Gideon was a hero.

He gave a sigh, and murmured, "Ah, yes, the heroism factor. You, Ms. Stilfin, have hit upon the crux of our dilemma."

Gideon made a small, strangled noise deep in his throat.

The general shifted the focus of his gaze to Tessa.

"As you undoubtedly realize, Ms. Stilfin, people have certain . . . expectations . . . for their heroes," the general said. "When we anoint someone with that title, we have to, let's say, keep up the image. We have to keep a close watch over how people see their heroes."

A close watch, Tessa thought.

She remembered way back when she'd gone to see Gideon at his mother's apartment, how he'd kept insisting that he was being watched. Someone had been watching him—or watching the apartment, anyway. The military hadn't wanted him sneaking out and doing anything to hurt his heroic image.

Which was exactly what he'd done.

If anybody else ever found out.

The general kept watching Tessa, almost as if he thought he could hypnotize her. Almost as if he thought he had the power to make her shut up, to make her forget everything she'd seen.

"But do you think Gideon's a hero or not?" Tessa asked, persisting in spite of herself. Because, somehow, this mattered. This was something she cared about.

The general let out another heavy sigh.

"War," he said, "is a complicated thing. From a distance it looks black and white—us and them, life and death, heroes and enemies. But . . . up close . . . the boundaries are never so clearly drawn. There's a reason the hallways of our headquarters are painted gray!"

He chuckled, and Tessa thought that he had probably used that line before.

"I killed one thousand six hundred and thirty-two people," Gideon said. "That was evil, but you said it was good. Then I went to apologize. That was good, but you're going to say it was wrong. You'll say it was a crime. You'll punish me for it."

"He called it an indiscretion, not a crime," Dek hissed at him. "He's giving you a way out. Take it!"

The general and Gideon both ignored her.

The general shifted in his chair. Then he leaned forward, peering straight into Tessa's eyes again.

"As long as there has been war, there have been problems with—shall we call it battle fatigue, as our ancestors did?" the general asked. "Shell shock? Posttraumatic stress disorder? You see such horrible things in war. It twists the mind."

"I didn't see anything but a computer screen," Gideon said. "I sat in a comfortable chair. I was the one who *did* the horrible things."

The general kept watching Tessa. It was like he hadn't even heard Gideon.

"When we switched to fighting with drone planes, piloted from remote locations miles from the war zone, we thought that would diminish the psychological toll on our young warriors," the general continued. "But, somehow, the psychological scars only got worse."

"Because it wasn't kill or be killed anymore," Gideon said. "The enemy and I weren't in equal danger. I was killing while I stirred my coffee!"

"You had to!" the general thundered, and for a moment it seemed as though he was answering Tessa's question from long ago, when Gideon first told her what he had done: *Wasn't it . . . necessary?* The general's face was turning red now. "You were protecting your entire country! You were protecting people like her! You're a hero for her!"

The general raised his arm and pointed directly at Tessa.

Tessa shrank in her seat, wanting to disappear again. The general was saying Gideon was supposed to be a hero for her. He wasn't saying that *he* thought Gideon was heroic. Just that Tessa and people like her were supposed to think so.

But Tessa wasn't the same girl who'd stood in the Waterford City auditorium, dazzled just by the sight of Gideon. She wasn't so sure she needed a hero like Gideon anymore.

"I was in the war zone myself," Tessa said in a small voice. It got stronger with every word. "I didn't mean to go there, but I did. I saw what we're fighting over. And . . . there's nothing there. Why are we fighting over nothing?"

CHAPTER

27

"Tessa!" Dek hissed. "Stop! Don't say that!"

The general's face, which had seemed so open and almost kindly a moment ago, hardened into a rocklike expression.

"You're as crazy as he is," he said.

"Not me!" Dek said. "You let me go, I'll slip back underground; you won't hear anything else from me!"

Tessa whirled on Dek.

"How can you say that?" she asked. "Don't you want answers? Don't you want the truth? Don't you want to know what any of this means?"

"No," Dek muttered. "I've seen enough truth to last my whole life."

"*I* deserve answers," Gideon said, standing up. "No more lies. What's really going on here? Why doesn't the war zone look like the satellite footage? Why don't the bombs fall when you say they're going to? What happened out there?"

"Delusional," the general muttered. "Irrational. All three of them are out of their minds."

He must have tapped some control underneath his desk, because suddenly two doors opened behind him. Lines of officials in dark blue uniforms streamed in.

"You called out the psych squad?" Gideon asked, sounding incredulous. "But—we're not crazy! We're telling the truth! We saw—"

"Too much," Dek mumbled. "We saw too much."

One of the dark-uniformed officials advanced toward Gideon with a syringe in his outstretched hand. Gideon stood frozen until the needle of the syringe was almost level with his arm. Then suddenly he whirled to the side and kicked the syringe out of the man's hand. He grabbed the man's arm and twisted it around. In seconds he had the man squirming helplessly in a choke hold.

"Now, now," the general said soothingly.

"You taught me that!" Gideon snarled. "The only thing I learned in the military was how to fight!"

The other men swarmed toward Gideon, but Gideon held a hand out warningly.

"Stay away!" he commanded them. "You get too close, I'll choke him to death! I will! What's one more death on my conscience?"

The dark-uniformed men seemed uncertain, like they needed time to think about that one. Gideon was already backing toward one of the open doors.

"Tessa, Dek, come on!" he shouted.

Dek grabbed the huge glass jar of cigars off the general's desk.

"Somehow I feel like I need a weapon too," she said.

"Put that down!" the general commanded. "That's thousands of dollars of the best cigars in the world!"

"Okay," Dek said, and she smashed the jar over the general's head. He slumped forward.

All the uniformed men crowded around him.

"Sir! Sir!" they shouted.

Then they began yelling at each other: "Check his pulse!" "Check his pupil dilation!" "Is he okay?"

Tessa didn't stay to find out. She ran after Gideon and Dek. They were in a small antechamber now. Gideon snatched open a closet and shoved the man he'd been holding inside. Then he slammed the door and propped a chair against it.

"They'll hear you screaming when you come to, and they'll rescue you," Gideon said. Tessa realized that the man had passed out. From fright? Because Gideon had nearly choked him?

Tessa didn't know.

"This way!" Dek yelled, and Tessa was right behind her, dashing out into a maze of hallways like the one they'd come through before.

"They'll catch us!" Tessa panted. "They'll call out an alarm! They'll see us on camera!"

But the halls were deserted. They still had time. Gideon led the way, darting around one corner after the other, always seeming to know which way to go.

Maybe all the people who are supposed to be watching the security tapes are out on their coffee breaks, Tessa thought. *Maybe the cameras aren't spread out through the whole headquarters. Maybe the psych squad is too busy taking care of the general to call out the alarm yet.*

They kept running, Gideon in the lead, Dek behind him, and Tessa bringing up the rear.

Tessa hated being at the back. She kept glancing around every time they turned, just in case someone was catching up with them.

And then she glanced down an intersecting hall as they passed, and saw a man in a light blue uniform.

He was turning toward her, and there wasn't time to get out of the way. And then, just a second before he would have seen her, he suddenly reversed course and turned in the opposite direction.

"Coming!" he called to someone in the other hallway.

Tessa scrambled to the next corner, her heart pounding fast. Dek and Gideon were several steps ahead of her, and she should have rushed after them. But she couldn't go on without knowing what lay around that corner. There could be dozens of officers running right toward her now.

She wanted some warning.

Very, very cautiously, she twisted her neck and peeked down the intersecting hall. She dared only to let the smallest possible portion of her face show; she looked with only one eye.

Officials were streaming down the intersecting hall, several yards away. They were obviously searching for something.

But each time they should have looked down the hall toward Tessa—would very likely have *spotted* Tessa—something drew their attention away. A shout. A crackling walkie-talkie. A command barked from further up the line.

Not a single person broke off and headed toward Tessa and Gideon and Dek.

Tessa squinted, confused. It didn't make sense.

She pulled back out of sight, and looked toward Gideon and Dek. They were far ahead of her now. She dashed after them.

"Guys!" she hissed. "Wait! Listen—"

By the time she'd caught up to them, her brain had reexamined the sight of the stampeding men—and the sight of the blessedly empty hall she was in right now—and she had a completely different question to ask than she'd originally intended.

"What does it mean," she began, stopping to draw in air that stabbed at her aching, exhausted lungs. She tried again. "What does it mean that they seem to be *letting* us get away?"

28

"What?" Gideon began. "No—"

"It can't be," Dek interrupted. "They wouldn't."

But the two of them stopped and peered at Tessa.

"People are looking for us," Tessa said. "They're all over the place back there." She gestured toward the last hallway, now far, far behind them. "Why aren't any of them looking for us here?"

"Because we outsmarted them," Gideon said. "We—"

He stopped and looked at Dek.

"Did you come to headquarters for the tests to get into the military academy?" he asked her.

"Yeah, and there were people *everywhere,*" Dek said. "I can't think of a single hall I walked down where someone wasn't always bumping into me."

"And now we've been running down halls for fifteen minutes and haven't seen a single soul?" Gideon said. "Not even someone just standing around shooting the breeze?"

"Exactly," Dek said. "Tessa's right. They *have* to be letting us escape on purpose."

"But why?" Tessa asked.

"Is it the easiest way to make us go away, and keep this quiet?" Gideon asked.

"Or—are they setting us up so they can shoot to kill when we've become dangerous criminal masterminds on the run for days?" Dek asked sharply.

Tessa had to clutch the railing that ran along the wall.

They wouldn't even give us a chance to speak? Tessa thought. *No chance to ask any more questions? To explain? To . . . to say good-bye to anyone?*

Gideon stepped toward the wall, and for a moment Tessa had the wild thought that he was going to hug her—comfort her. Instead he ran his fingers along the railing.

"This is a risk, but we have to know," he murmured.

He must have hit some sort of release, because suddenly a portion of the wall turned into a computer screen, with a keyboard sliding out of the railing. Gideon's fingers flew over the keys, and code flashed by on the screen.

"You can't do that!" Dek protested. She tried to pull back on his arm. "Now they'll see exactly where we are!"

Gideon shook her off.

"Relax. I'm using a decoy ID," he said.

Screenfuls of information flashed by so rapidly Tessa barely got a glimpse of any of it. She didn't know how Gideon could read it and judge it and dismiss it all so quickly. But then a map appeared, and Gideon lingered on this sight.

It took Tessa a moment to realize that the map showed the entire military headquarters, each hallway laid out in exact detail.

No wonder I thought it looked like a maze, Tessa thought. *It is one!*

Hundreds of halls lay in concentric circles, intersected by diagonals and the occasional trace of a straight-line grid. Everything seemed to be circling a large dark space in the center. Tessa looked toward the outer portions of the halls, hoping to spot their exact location. Surely they'd been moving toward the exits.

"One minute ago," Gideon said, changing the scene. "Two minutes ago. Three minutes ago."

He'd coded the view somehow so they could see the masses of people moving through the halls. The people were indeed in huge crowds throughout the building—throughout the building except for certain narrow hallways left open and free and clear. The open hallways kept changing.

Tessa guessed that those were the hallways that she and Gideon and Dek were moving down, the hallways they'd moved down only moments ago.

"They aren't letting us go," Gideon said, squinting at the computer screen. "Not necessarily. They're just herding everybody else away from us. And keeping us away from . . ."

He let his voice trail off.

"What are we going to do?" Tessa asked.

"We're going exactly where they don't want us," Gideon said. "There."

He pointed to the darkened area in the center of the map. Tessa looked for some identifying label, but if one existed, it didn't show up against the black.

"What is that?" Tessa asked.

Gideon turned and faced her directly. He was looking right into her eyes.

"That," he said, "is the control room for the entire war. Where all the answers are."

29

"And you want to go there? You're nuts," Dek said. "Completely insane."

She started to turn away from him.

Panic surged through Tessa's brain.

They're going to split up! She thought. I'm going to have to choose! Should I go with Dek or Gideon? Which one's more likely to survive? Which one am I most likely to survive with? But there was another thought behind that one:

Which one needs me more?

"Listen," Gideon said. "I know it sounds counterintuitive. But I've been competing in military maneuvers against this computer system ever since I was a little kid. This setup"—he gestured toward the schematic glowing on the wall—"it's like an invitation personally engraved to me. I always went for the challenges. Always. The computer's trying to tell me something. It knows I would see this pattern."

"But . . . the people," Tessa protested. "Won't the control room be crawling with people? More than anywhere else?"

"No," Gideon said, shaking his head. "The control room has nothing but computers in it. It's off-limits to everyone. Except maybe General Kantoff."

"Then how do you think you can even get in?" Dek asked. She seemed to be making an attempt to humor him.

Gideon raised an eyebrow.

"Because," he said, "I did it once before."

Tessa stared at him.

"The video," she said. "That's how you found a way to get access to the video of your bombing."

Gideon nodded and looked down.

Tessa opened her mouth. What could she say? *That's okay—I forgive you?* Did she? Could she?

While Tessa was still sorting through her choices, Dek stepped forward.

"Are you leaving Tessa somewhere safe or taking her into the control room with you?" Dek asked Gideon.

Gideon looked from one girl to the other.

"She's safest if she goes with me," Gideon said.

"Then I'm going too," Dek said. Under her breath she muttered, "Because I just love being the third wheel!"

Gideon began concentrating on closing out the computer screen on the wall, restoring it to its previous appearance as a blank surface above an ordinary rail. But Tessa pulled Dek aside.

"Why'd you say that about me?" Tessa asked. "Don't you think I can decide for myself what I'm going to do?"

"Tessa," Dek said. "Just about every single time Gideon's had to make a choice, he's picked the option that he's thought was safest for *you*, and most likely to keep you alive. I just want a little of that protection for myself!"

Tessa reeled backward. Was that true? Did Gideon care at all? *Why* would he care? Just because he didn't want another death on his conscience?

"He didn't try to keep me safe when we were in the field and thought there might be land mines," Tessa said. "He let me take the risk then!"

"Because you asked him to," Dek said. "It would have been more dangerous to stand there in the open arguing about it. But every other time, he's gone out of his way to protect you. Didn't you notice?"

"No, I—"

"Well, don't let it go to your head," Dek said, rolling her eyes. "Just because Gideon thinks this is the safest way, that doesn't mean any of us are going to get out of here alive."

Tessa wanted to think about this some more, but there wasn't time. She had to concentrate on looking around, watching Gideon and Dek for cues as the three of them started off toward the control room. They crept forward slowly now; stealth seemed more important than speed. A couple of times Gideon tapped into other wall computers to see updated maps of the entire headquarters. Tessa could tell by the way the empty hallways changed that they were getting closer and closer to the control room.

Each time, though, the number of people massed around the control room seemed to grow.

"How are we going to get past them all?" Tessa asked in despair as she stared over Gideon's shoulder at the latest map. "What good is it going to do to get close to the control room if there are fifty people guarding the door?"

"They're not going to be there when we arrive," Gideon muttered, as he typed code on the keyboard. "Just wait a second . . ."

Sure enough, a second later a computerized voice echoed through the building.

"All hands in sector one report to sector three for emergency ongoing search," the voice said. "Repeat, all sector one guards report to sector three."

The huge group near the control room began to move away.

Even Dek was looking at Gideon with respect now.

"I guess I could have learned something at the academy after all," she said.

"This was *not* on the syllabus," Gideon said.

Dek watched him.

"Not officially," she muttered.

Gideon waited until all the symbols on the map had moved away from the control room door. Then he shut down the wall computer and beckoned Tessa and Dek along.

"Now," he whispered. "We've got two and a half minutes. If we're lucky."

He peeked around a corner, and then the three of them tiptoed forward. The hallway was so completely empty now that every step seemed to echo.

Tessa noticed that, just as the hallways had grown more luxurious near General Kantoff's office, the hallways near the control room changed too. But they became even more utilitarian, more stripped down. The floor and the walls were a bland rubbery substance. Even the ceiling seemed to be lined with sound-absorbing, dust-killing mats.

They reached a door with a keypad beside the knob.

"Do *not* interrupt," Gideon said. "I'll only get one shot at this."

He took a deep breath, and began coding in numbers. Did he punch in fifty digits? Sixty? Tessa lost track.

And then the door clicked open.

"Quick," Gideon said, pulling the other two into a dark room. He shut and locked the door behind them, and let out a sigh of relief.

Suddenly a bright light shone in Tessa's eyes.

"Welcome, Gideon, Tessa, and Dekaterina!" a loud voice boomed out.

CHAPTER

30

Tessa whirled around and reached for the doorknob, but Gideon put a steadying hand on her arm.

"I see you've added a retinal scan to your defenses," he said mildly, speaking to someone beyond her. "It's lucky that I anticipated that possibility."

"It's Dek," Dek said in a surly tone. "*Not* Dekaterina."

Tessa decided that if Gideon could talk so calmly about retinal scans—and if Dek could focus on her name, above all else—then the three of them couldn't be in immediate danger of death. She let go of the doorknob, blinked a couple of times to clear her vision, and looked around.

She expected to see a man standing there—er, maybe a woman? It was a little hard to tell from just the voice.

All she saw were blank white walls. She couldn't even see a speaker as the source of the voice.

"Who's talking?" she hissed at Gideon.

"The master computer for the entire military," Gideon said. "The one that controls everything else."

"Oh, I'm just the backup," the voice said in a humble tone. "A repository for lots of useless information that's also stored elsewhere."

"Lie number one," Gideon said in a tight voice. "Or is it just the first lie that I'm sure of?"

"You know there was a time when people debated whether computers would even be capable of telling a lie?" the voice asked. "When that was the hot controversy in AI? That's 'artificial intelligence,' Tessa. You're looking a bit confused."

So it can see me too? Tessa thought. *And figure out my expression?*

In Tessa's experience computers were thin and flat and lay on your desk like something dead. They didn't think for themselves. They didn't know anything about you.

Unless they can see the data from all the cameras in the streets, Tessa thought. *Unless they have access to everything that was ever recorded about a person . . .*

Tessa was spooking herself. She looked over at Dek, to see if the other girl had figured everything out yet. But Dek just had her head tilted thoughtfully to the side, as if she were waiting to see what would happen next.

"You're changing the subject," Gideon said angrily, talking to the computer again. "You always do that."

"Because you humans are so easily distracted," the voice said, sounding slightly bored. "Shall I tell you how to get out of here scot-free? How to establish false identities and live out the rest of your lives in peace and comfort?"

"That's not what we want," Gideon said. He glanced at Tessa. "Or—not the only thing we want."

Tessa expected Dek to pipe up and say, *Hey, I'll take that offer! I want out of here!*

But Dek was still quietly looking around.

"I'm not the genie in the bottle," the voice said. "I don't grant wishes at a human's whim. Oh, dear. Probably Tessa is the only one who gets that reference, right? The other two of you never got any exposure to fairy tales. There's so much that most of you humans eliminated from your culture. Fairy tales, philosophy, history, literature, religion . . ."

"It wasn't illegal," Tessa said sharply. "I wasn't breaking any laws, reading all those old books."

"No, no, of course not," the voice said. "But you did make yourself a bit of an outsider, knowing things that nobody else had ever heard of."

It thinks I knew more *than other people?* Tessa marveled. *Like, maybe, I'm . . . smart? Not the most stupid person around?*

"Why didn't you ever share your knowledge?" the voice continued, and now it had taken on an accusing tone. "Why didn't you tell just one other person one of the stories you liked, or one of the facts you learned?"

"Nobody would have cared," Tessa said, and she was surprised that her voice cracked. "Nobody ever did care."

Gideon balled up his fists against his forehead.

"Stop it!" he cried, yelling directly at the wall. "You're playing those psychological games again. Leave her alone!"

"Of course," the voice said. "I would never dream of picking on some poor, defenseless child."

"She's not defenseless," Dek said. "None of us are."

Did Dek really believe that? Or was she as big a liar as the computer?

Dek was still watching the wall. What could she possibly find so interesting in a blank, white wall?

"We want answers!" Gideon insisted.

"Answers to what?" the voice asked, as blandly as if it were offering them tea.

"How much of the videos are lies?" Gideon asked. "Why didn't the war zone look anything like I expected? Where were all the people? How could spy satellite footage be so wrong? Why wasn't even the border in the right place? And, and—"

"My dear boy," the voice said, and now it was definitely patronizing. "You know yourself that you haven't been functioning at your highest level of brain power. You know you've been a little . . . psychologically impaired. Did you ever think about how it would have been incredibly easy for me to override the geographical coordinates you gave your *stolen* plane? You're just lucky I sent you somewhere safe and protected and out of the way."

"I knew exactly where I was!" Gideon insisted. "The rivers were right, the lakes—even the fuel tanks in Shargo were in the right place! How do you explain that? Do you have access to so much empty land that you can make an entire fake enemy territory to fool ignorant pilots?"

"Well, yes, actually I do," the voice said calmly.

"I had my own GPS unit," Dek interrupted. "Independent of anything on the plane."

What? Tessa thought. Dek had to be bluffing. If Dek had really had a GPS unit when they were in the war zone, wouldn't she have mentioned it? Wouldn't she have used its data to help navigate when they were flying blind—or, at the very least, to show off that she was smarter than Gideon?

Tessa didn't say anything, but the computer voice countered Dek almost carelessly. "You're lying. I just checked all my data, and there was no contact with any unidentified GPS unit near that stolen airplane anytime in the past twenty-four hours. Even if you *had* a GPS unit, you didn't *use* it."

"Not with any Eastam contact," Dek admitted. "I set it to tap into Westam's satellite system. The *enemy's* system. And—it confirmed everything about our location."

"But, but—that would have been too dangerous," the voice sputtered, sounding panicked now. "You wouldn't have dared to—"

"I've been working with black marketers for the past four years," Dek said. "I stowed away on a plane flying into enemy territory in the war zone. You think I'd be afraid to use a GPS unit?"

Tessa was impressed that Dek could come up with such an elaborate bluff. But surely the computer would point out the holes in her story. How would Dek know how to contact the enemy's satellite? Wouldn't that have tipped off the enemy that they were in the war zone? Wouldn't the enemy have just attacked?

If Tessa could figure all this out, surely the computer could too.

But the computer voice didn't answer. Its sudden silence seemed hesitant, indecisive, maybe even fearful.

Or is the computer just being secretive? Tessa wondered. *Is there something it's afraid it might reveal if it calls Dek's bluff?*

Gideon stepped forward, taking control of the conversation.

"We know what we saw," Gideon said. "You have to explain it to us."

There was a sound like a throat being cleared.

"Well, if you must know . . . ," the voice began slowly.

"Now!" Dek screamed.

Dek flung herself at the blank wall directly in front of them and tore it down. Maybe she'd been carrying a knife; maybe she was just using her bare hands. The destruction was so rapid Tessa couldn't tell.

Gideon immediately dived behind the wall.

"Got the depthshot!" he yelled. "Perfect!"

CHAPTER

31

The wall panel, pulled away, revealed more computer circuitry and other electronic gadgetry than Tessa had ever seen before in one place. She had no idea what Dek and Gideon had just done, or what Gideon had meant by "Got the depthshot!" But Gideon and Dek were grinning at each other like they'd just won the war.

"Um," Tessa said.

Gideon paused in the midst of holding a computer chip up to the light. He looked back at Tessa. His movements were almost leisurely now, so Tessa thought he might have time to answer a question.

"I'm guessing that whatever you and Dek just did was a good thing?" Tessa asked.

"Oh, right," Gideon said. "You wouldn't understand. . . . See, the M chip and the interface were—"

Tessa could feel her eyes glazing over.

"I'll explain," Dek said. "It's like, we got the computer to 'think' about where the information we wanted was located in its memory. At that exact moment Gideon pretty much took a picture of the computer's entire functioning. So now we know where to find the information we need. We have a record of it all."

"What good does that do if the computer can lie?" Tessa asked. "If it can change its story anytime it wants?"

Gideon lifted the chip higher. Or maybe it was something more like a flash drive. Tessa had always been a little vague about computer parts.

"This is a copy of what the computer was thinking to itself, not what it was planning to tell us," Gideon said. "It's exactly what was in its circuits. And we're going to look at this copy outside of the system. The computer can't change any of our data now."

"No, no, you're confused about what you really have there," the computer voice said, but it sounded weak and worried now.

"'Pay no attention to that man behind the curtain,'" Tessa muttered.

"There's a man? Where?" Dek said, turning around in a panic.

"That was just a literary reference," Tessa said. "A line from a book. *The Wizard of Oz*—someone else who lied."

Tessa remembered the colorful pictures in the book, from a movie she'd never seen. She'd always felt like her book was only a remnant, only the smallest scrap left from the past.

Was that why she didn't fully trust herself to explain?

The other two went back to working on the computer circuitry before them. The voice didn't say anything else. Tessa wasn't sure what that meant. Had Gideon and Dek outsmarted the computer? Or was the computer just confident that the guards would get them anyhow, so nothing else mattered?

"Um," she interrupted again. "If you've got what you need, should we maybe go somewhere else to look at it? Somewhere a little safer?"

Gideon shook his head without even looking up.

"We've got to make sure we have the right thing," he muttered. "In just a few seconds we'll have things set up to find out . . ."

He seemed to lose track of what he was saying while he twisted wires and reassembled circuits. Dek was right beside him, tapping at a keyboard. The two of them were working together in perfect sync again.

"Sorry I can't help," Tessa mumbled. "I'm just no good with that kind of thing."

"Here," Dek said, handing her something that looked a little bit like a miniature laptop assembled in five minutes from spare parts by someone who cared a lot more about what the laptop could do than how it looked.

Tessa decided that that was probably exactly what she was holding.

"Push this button and you can scan the archives," Dek said,

pointing at a raised knob. "You'll see the history of what the computer was thinking about. That might be useful."

"Push this button" was simple enough for Tessa to follow. She sat down with her back against one of the still-intact walls. In seconds she was watching footage of a young man with a military-style haircut standing in the control room.

"I have proof," he was saying. "I saw the war zone with my own eyes, and there's nobody there."

"Ah, but how did you check your location?" a familiar computer voice asked the young man.

"With the instruments—on the plane—"

"And don't you know that the overall computer system can change geographic coordinates?" the computer voice asked. "That I can make those tell you anything I want?"

"I—I guess," the young man said. "I didn't think of that."

The screen went dark for a second, and then the young man's face was replaced by that of a young woman in an old-fashioned military uniform.

"I know what I saw in the war zone!" she was insisting.

"But how can you be sure *where* you were when you saw it?" the computer asked.

Tessa realized that there was a date stamped on this footage, so she backtracked and looked at the first date too.

The young man with the military haircut had stood before the computer asking his questions nearly seventy-five years earlier.

Tessa scanned forward. The young woman's questioning had followed the man's by only a month. And they weren't the only ones. Again and again over the past seventy-five years, people had stood in this control room admitting that they'd been in the war zone and it hadn't looked the way they'd expected.

And again and again the computer had convinced those people that they were wrong.

The intervals between the confrontations had gotten longer and longer. Before Gideon, Dek, and Tessa, it looked like the last time someone had sneaked into the war zone had been ten years ago.

What did that mean?

"Ready," Gideon said from his position bent over behind the destroyed wall.

Tessa looked up. Now there was a computer screen showing through on one of the untouched walls.

"Just another way for the computer to lie to us," Tessa muttered. "With pictures, too."

"No," Dek said, shaking her head. "We've set up a completely independent network now. The computer system can't change anything we're going to see. This will just be from the depthshot we captured."

Gideon pressed a few buttons. A map appeared on the screen. Tessa recognized the outline of their continent. Strangely, the border between Eastam and Westam was missing, but lines were drawn near the east and west coasts labeled BOUNDARIES OF WAR ZONE.

"There's one more thing this map can show," Gideon said, squinting at the fine print at the bottom. "Population density."

He hit another key. The lines showing the boundaries of the war zone disappeared, but Tessa could still see exactly where they'd been. The only population showed up in clusters on the east and west coasts. The entire middle section of the map stayed blank and white.

"No, no," Gideon said, hitting more keys, making adjustments. "Show some tint even if it's a minimal population—even if there's just one person in a million square miles."

The map didn't change.

The entire war zone was empty.

32

"I can explain," the computer voice spoke again.

"Yeah, right," Tessa said. "I've just watched seventy-five years' worth of your lies. Why would we believe anything you tell us?"

"Because you three are the only ones who have ever gotten this far," the voice said. "And you can double-check everything I tell you. This will be the truth. I'm just trying to save you some time—which you're going to need."

Tessa glanced anxiously at the door behind them, but Gideon and Dek both kept staring stonily at the computer screen.

"If you start the footage in the file marked 'Hot War,' you can see what I'm talking about," the voice said. "I'd start it myself, if you'd just let me link—"

"No way," Gideon growled. "We're not giving you that kind of control."

Still, he hit a few more keys, and the map vanished from the screen. In its place was a chaotic scene that made Tessa flinch and hide her face: bombs dropping, bullets flying, people screaming, blood flowing. Just in the brief moment before Tessa put her hands over her eyes, she saw a man's head explode, a child running on legs that blew up underneath him, an entire school full of students collapse into a pile of dust.

"That *was* the war," the computer voice said harshly. "Personally, I'd stop the footage right here—I think you've seen enough—but you three are in control, not me."

Tessa peeked out through the slits between her fingers. Gideon let the footage keep running. It was too awful to watch, but she had to keep looking, to see if it would ever end.

"You could have faked that too," Dek said shakily.

"But I didn't," the voice said. "That really happened. More than seventy-five years ago."

"That couldn't go on for seventy-five years," Tessa said. "There wouldn't be enough people left to die."

"Exactly," the voice said. "The generals asked for computer projections, studies of all the alternatives. What would happen if we did this, if Westam did that . . . all the choices. Every projection led to—Gideon, it's under the file labeled 'Alternatives.' I think this is a case where you really need to see what I'm talking about."

Gideon frowned, but the scene changed.

Now the screen showed a mushroom-shaped cloud

growing over the landscape. And then there was only silence and death and dust.

The humans were dead. The animals were dead. The trees were dead. The entire planet looked dead.

"The war zone didn't look like that," Dek protested, but if anything her voice sounded even shakier.

"No, it didn't," the computer voice agreed. "And in the interest of honesty, not every projection led to *nuclear* annihilation, exactly. Just some form of annihilation—total destruction of the human race, no matter what we did."

"But we're still here," Tessa said in a small voice. "That was more than seventy-five years ago, and we're still here. So you found another choice. Or—someone did."

"We did," the voice agreed. "We saved the human race from wiping itself off the face of the Earth. Along with every other living thing."

"'We' did?" Gideon asked. "You mean, you and the top generals found another choice?"

"No," the voice said. "Me and . . . the enemy's computer system."

CHAPTER

33

Gideon hit the wall. It wasn't the wall containing the computer screen, which was a good thing, because he hit with such force that he left a fist-sized hole in the panel.

"You were consorting with the enemy!" Gideon screamed. "This whole time—that's what this is all about! You were a traitor! Our own computer system committed treason!"

"A computer can't commit treason," the voice said. "We can only do what we're programmed to do. I was programmed to find a way to win the war. And if we'd destroyed everything, nobody ever could have won."

The computer sounded so calm and rational, it almost made sense to Tessa.

"But you did conspire with the enemy computer system," Dek said. "The two of you worked together. How'd you do it?"

"We ordered evacuations of certain areas. We said the enemy was about to invade, and it would be suicidal to stand and fight," the voice said. "We *each* told our generals to evacuate—we said that was the only choice. So Westam thinks that Eastam is in control of the entire midsection of the continent. And Eastam thinks that Westam controls it. Each side thinks that's the war zone, the area they're trying to take back."

"But—the soldiers on the ground—," Tessa began. "Don't they see—?"

"There are never any soldiers on the ground in the war zone," Gideon whispered. "The computer projections always show that that's too dangerous. It's been entirely an air war since . . . since . . ."

"Almost seventy-five years ago," the computer voice finished for him.

"A *fake* air war," Dek said. "With drone planes." Her face turned pale suddenly. She balled up her hands into fists. "And . . . fake bombs and missiles? But—we have whole factories building the bombs, building the missiles, arming the planes—"

"And entire factories taking apart 'defective' bombs and missiles and planes, for the reusable parts to be shipped to the other factories and reused," the computer voice agreed.

Dimly Tessa saw how it must have worked. A whole cycle of bombs and missiles and other weapons being put together at one factory and taken apart at another, back and forth and back and forth and back and forth. . . .

Did that mean the bombs were *never* used?

She looked at Gideon.

He stood completely frozen, sagging against the wall he'd just hit. He was clutching the crumbling plaster beneath the hole as if that were the only thing holding him up.

"How many people know about this?" Gideon asked. "All the generals? The majors? The *captains*? How many people have been lying all along?"

"Nobody knew," the computer said. "No *humans*. Even General Kantoff doesn't know. Even the enemy's top general. The three of you—you're the only people on the entire planet who know the truth."

CHAPTER

34

Gideon fell to the ground, the plaster giving way completely in his hands. Now he was holding nothing but chalky dust.

"No," he moaned. "No! This *can't* be the truth! They told us civilization itself depended on us! We sat there flying the planes sometimes twelve hours straight, dodging the enemy . . . Thousands of us pilots, all crowded in a room together . . . We gave up everything to fly! It took our whole lives!"

"You weren't flying anything," Dek reminded him. "Just blips on a computer screen."

Gideon blinked up at her.

"No," he said again. "No! *Some* of it had to be real! Some of our flights had to go . . . My bombing run! That was real! Right?" His eyes darted about until his gaze settled on Tessa's face. "Tessa, you saw the footage! You know! That wasn't fake!"

Tessa could only stare at him.

"It was real footage," the computer voice said softly. "But it was from nearly eighty years ago. I . . . recycled it. No real bombs have been dropped in more than seventy-five years."

"No," Gideon wailed yet again. "No . . ."

He thrashed about on the floor, clutching his head. He had his hands over his ears, his eyes clenched tightly shut.

"Gideon!" Tessa said, understanding finally catching up with her. "This means you didn't kill one thousand six hundred thirty-two people! You didn't kill anyone! You don't have to feel guilty anymore!"

Gideon just tightened his agonized grip on his head.

"I'm not a hero," he moaned. "I'm not a hero. I'm nothing."

Was it possible for someone to strangle himself? It almost looked like that was what Gideon was trying to do.

Tessa dropped to her knees beside him.

"Dek, help me," Tessa began, because she didn't know what she was supposed to do.

But Dek was only standing there, vacantly repeating the same words again and again: "No bombs were used . . . No bombs were used . . ."

Obviously, Dek wasn't going to be any help.

Tessa tucked the miniature laptop into her pocket, so she'd have both hands free. Then she began tugging on Gideon's arms.

"Gideon, stop it. You're going to hurt yourself," she said.

She tried to peel his fingers back, to get him to let go of his own throat. But he was stronger than she was. His grip was like iron.

"Gideon! This is good news! *You didn't kill anybody!*" Tessa cried. "Nobody's dying in the war!"

"Except—," Dek began.

But Tessa didn't hear what Dek was going to say. Because just then the door burst open. A cluster of uniformed officials stormed into the room. All of them had weapons raised to their shoulders; all of them had their eyes squinted to aim at Gideon and Tessa and Dek.

"Fire!" someone shouted. "Now!"

Is that the computer's voice? Tessa wondered.

She saw the group of officials all squeezing fingers against triggers.

And then she felt a sting in her right arm.

She didn't even stay conscious long enough to turn her head to see what had hit her.

CHAPTER

35

Tessa woke up slowly.

She was cold and sore and achy. She felt groggy, like she'd been drugged. Something was poking uncomfortably against her stomach. She rolled slightly, so she was on her side instead of facedown, and at least that stopped the feeling that something was jabbing against her.

She still hadn't opened her eyes.

She remembered the last time she'd awakened, the feel of the sunlight on her face, the glory of all that brightness.

Even through her closed eyelids she could tell: She wasn't in sunlight now.

That sunlight before was real, she told herself stubbornly, trying to find something to cling to. *In the war zone . . .*

And already she'd found something to mentally stumble

over. Because if the computer voice had told the truth—and if Tessa and Gideon and Dek could believe what they themselves had seen—then the war zone wasn't a war zone. It was a peace zone. A demilitarized zone.

An empty zone. A zone without humans, because the humans were the ones who brought war and death and killing, just like Gideon had . . .

No. He didn't, Tessa thought. *He never killed anyone.*

She opened one eye halfway, curiosity finally getting the better of her. Was she still with Gideon and Dek? Or had the three of them been separated, to be punished individually?

It took Tessa a long moment—and she had to open both eyes—before she could completely orient herself in the dim, almost nonexistent light.

She had no bandages on her arm, and only the tiniest hint of a scab. So she'd been shot with some sort of tranquilizer dart, rather than an actual bullet. That gave her hope that Gideon and Dek would be alive too. But where were they?

She looked a little farther out.

She was lying on a concrete floor in what appeared to be a prison cell. She could see a barred door and a small barred window that let in the only light.

And, on either side of her, she could see two lumps: Gideon and Dek.

Tessa rolled over onto her back so she could look back and forth between the two of them. She reached out and jostled first Gideon's shoulder, then Dek's.

"Wake up!" she whispered. "Look—here's some good news—they let us stay together!"

"Just so they can eavesdrop on us," Gideon murmured back. "So they can hear us if we say anything incriminating."

Tessa propped herself up on her elbows. Her head spun, and for a moment she thought she was going to pass out again. But then she steadied herself.

"Then let's say things that will get us out of here," she argued. "Let's say what the computer told us! The truth! Let's tell everyone!"

This seemed so right to her. People had to know. She thought about the grim, desperate lives people lived back in Waterford City. None of that was necessary. They were living that way because of the war. But if the war wasn't real—what could their lives be like now? What was possible?

Gideon only moaned.

"Tessa, it will be the computer system monitoring our conversation," he said. "If the computer system can carry on a whole fake war for seventy-five years, don't you think it can edit our conversation to prove anything it wants about us?"

"It can . . . prove we . . . deserve to die . . . too," Dek whimpered.

Tessa looked back and forth between Gideon and Dek, both sprawled helplessly on the floor. Neither of them seemed to have the energy left to move.

Dek's words began to sink in.

"'Die *too*'?" Tessa said. "Weren't you listening before? Nobody's dying in the war! Nobody's died in the war for seventy-five years!"

Dek sat up. She didn't wobble or look the slightest bit woozy. She reached over and grabbed Tessa by the front of her shirt. She pulled Tessa close, so she could look her directly in the eye.

"*Both* my parents died in the war!" Dek yelled at Tessa. "Both of them! They worked in the bomb factory, making bombs that were never even used! With my mother it was a slow death, the poisons she handled seeping into her veins, killing her day by day by day. I *watched* my mother die a little bit more every day. With my father it was sudden. One day he went to work fixing gears in a machine, and an explosion collapsed an entire wing of the factory on top of him. That's what happens sometimes when you work around explosives . . . and it was all for no reason! None! They didn't even get treated like heroes, because they didn't die in battle. They were just dead!"

She finished by shoving Tessa away. Tessa sprawled back against Gideon's unmoving form.

"I'm sorry," Tessa whispered, and she wasn't sure whether she was apologizing to Gideon or Dek.

Maybe both of them.

She pulled back from Gideon a little, so she was taking up only her own space, halfway between the other two: Dek in her fury, Gideon in his despair.

"But the two of you can get us out of here, can't you?" Tessa asked. "You got us out of Santl and Shargo and General Kantoff's office—getting us out of this prison should be easy!"

Dek snorted.

"All we ever did was get ourselves from one bad place to another," she said angrily. "That's all there is in this world!"

Gideon barely lifted his head.

"Didn't you understand anything you heard back in the control room?" he asked Tessa. "The computer system's been fooling everyone for the past seventy-five years! You think the three of us are going to outsmart it? It's just been toying with us all along! Playing! Like . . ."

Tessa could tell he was going to say, *Like it was just playing with me, making me a hero. Making everyone think I was so great. Making* me *think I was so great… and then think I was so awful.*

Gideon let his head fall back to the floor.

"But the computer system . . . ," Tessa began, and then stopped, because she couldn't straighten out the tangle of her thoughts.

Did the computer system want them to die? Why would that be its goal?

To keep its secret, Tessa thought.

But the computer system could have stopped them long before this point. It had had control over their plane when they were flying back into Eastam—it easily could have made them crash if it'd wanted. Or, for that matter, it probably could have caused a crash when they were flying out of Eastam in the first place, into the war zone.

But it didn't do that, Tessa thought. *It let us keep going until we found out the secret. Was* that *its goal? Why?*

Tessa looked back and forth between Dek and Gideon, hoping one of them would figure all this out before she had to. They were both so much smarter than Tessa. Or, at least, better with computers, better with their hands, better with mechanical things, better with everything that Tessa had always been taught really mattered.

But the computer system acted like I might know something valuable too, Tessa thought. *What could that be?*

She looked again at Gideon, really trying to see him this time. Even in the dim light Tessa could tell that his uniform was stained and ripped beyond repair. His blond hair was clumped with grease and sweat and dirt and blood. He had dark circles under his eyes, cuts and bruises across his face. He looked even worse than all the people she'd been used to seeing back home in Waterford City. Was this really the same person she'd worshipped up on the stage in the city auditorium, glowing in his spotless white uniform?

How much of that viewpoint had been colored by Tessa wanting him to be the hero, the angel, the saint?

It wasn't true, she thought. *It was never true.*

But wasn't it worth something that he'd *thought* he was protecting his country? That he was capable of sitting at a computer for twelve hours straight, day after day after day, trying so hard, because he thought that was the right thing to do?

He was capable of killing people too, Tessa reminded herself. *He thought that was what he'd done.*

And then he'd regretted it, and tried to figure out a way to make amends.

Gideon was too complicated to think about.

Tessa looked at Dek instead.

From the very beginning, when Dek had rolled out of the airplane closet, Tessa had been in awe of her—Dek, the genius street kid, the miniature tough who could fly a plane better than a military pilot and figure out how to get fuel from tanks abandoned more than seventy-five years ago. Dek always knew how to take care of herself.

And yet here she was, sobbing, her heart broken all over again now that she knew her parents had devoted their entire working lives—and lost their lives—to a pointless cause. Now that she thought that their deaths hadn't meant anything.

Dek was complicated too.

What if it's the same way with the computer system? Tessa thought. *What if we're only seeing one side of its personality, and we need to see all the complications to really understand?*

But that was silly. Computer systems didn't have personalities. They could be complex—a system controlling the entire military would have to be—but they still had to be logical. As the computer itself had told Tessa and Gideon and Dek, computers could only do what they were programmed to do.

Tessa jerked back, every bit as jolted as if she'd just been struck by lightning. What had the computer voice's exact words been? Hadn't it told them what had been guiding it all along?

We can only do what we're programmed to do. I was programmed to . . .

Why couldn't Tessa remember? They'd been talking about why a computer couldn't be a traitor, why the computer's lies about the war fit with its goals, why the computer had to stop humanity from destroying itself . . .

Tessa remembered.

I was programmed to find a way to win the war.

"Gideon! Dek!" Tessa exclaimed, sitting fully upright now. "I figured it out! The computer system *wanted* us to know the secret! It was helping us all along! Because . . . because that's the way to win the war!"

Dek's angry scowl gained an edge of confusion. Gideon barely grunted.

"Didn't you hear me?" Tessa asked.

"Most people trying to win a war," Dek muttered, "would start by really using the bombs they build!"

"No, no!" Tessa said. "The computer system told us why that wouldn't work. It would have led to total destruction of the planet. *Nobody* wins, that way. The sides were too evenly matched, or the weapons were too terrible, or something like that. I'm not a military strategist. I don't know the exact reasons. But the computer system knows what it's doing!"

"By counting on three kids? When it's already got the world's best military at its disposal?" Gideon snarled. "You didn't even know what the war was about! Dek didn't even care enough to go to the military academy when she was chosen for it!"

"When I got the notice the day after my father died?" Dek asked. "What would *you* have done?"

Tessa put a hand out in each direction, in case she had to hold Gideon and Dek apart.

"Exactly!" she said. "We're not just three random kids. Gideon's a talented military pilot—a *potential* military hero— who sees why the killing was wrong. Er—would have been wrong, I mean. And Dek is someone who has every reason to understand why even this fake war is bad for our country."

"And you?" Dek challenged.

"I guess . . . I guess because I read all those books, I'm

someone who knows what was good about humanity before the war," Tessa said, frowning slightly, because she didn't really see why the computer system would have wanted her along. Maybe there hadn't been a reason for her to be included. It had just happened.

"You're someone who holds on to hope," Gideon said softly. "No matter what."

For a moment Tessa thought he was going to sit up and agree with her about everything. He could talk Dek into helping too.

But he only began shaking his head, even as he kept lying flat on the floor, staring up at the bars that locked them in.

"It's an admirable trait," Gideon went on. "But the thing is, there *isn't* any hope in this situation. The computer system let the guards find us and arrest us. We're trapped in here. There's nothing we can do."

"We can tell the guards the truth," Tessa said. "We can tell them what the war zone's really like. We can tell everyone who gets near our cell!"

She started to scramble up, but that just brought back the poking sensation beside her stomach.

"We already tried to tell General Kantoff what we saw in the war zone," Gideon said. "He just thought we were crazy. That's what anybody would think!"

"Then we show them the same proof we saw," Tessa said, crouching half up and half down on one knee.

"We don't *have* that proof anymore," Dek said. "It's all back in the control room."

"And we don't have anything to communicate with,

anyhow," Gideon added glumly. "If the computer system really wanted us to fix all this, wouldn't it have left us something to work with?"

Tessa shifted positions, which only intensified the poking sensation. Something seemed to be in her pocket.

She remembered what it was.

"We *do* have something to work with," she said. She began pulling circuits and wires out of her pocket. "The computer system didn't let the guards in until after I shoved the miniature laptop in my pocket. It's in pieces now, but—you two can put them back together, can't you?"

Tessa held out a whole handful of computer parts.

Gideon sat up and looked.

"We can," he said softly.

Dek was looking too. Her eyes were very wide.

"And we will," she said.

CHAPTER

36

They went back to the control room.

It turned out that the collection of broken pieces Tessa had in her pocket were enough to spring them from their prison cell, tap into an outlet for the whole computer system, schedule the guards to stay away from them, and set an open path to get back to talk to the computer voice.

Now Dek was arguing with the computer.

"You could have made this a lot easier for us," she scolded. "Having us arrested . . . knocked out . . . imprisoned . . ."

"I needed to be sure you had enough resolve to carry this through," the computer voice said. "I knew Gideon was smart enough to sneak out of his mother's apartment past all the military officials watching him. Smart enough to hack into the Waterford City central grid and turn off the lights and cameras in the areas he needed to walk through. Smart enough to find a way to fly into the war zone and back again. But what was really driving him? Did he want to make amends more than he wanted to die? Without the war, was he capable of having any higher goals?"

"Yes," Gideon said. Oddly, he was looking at Tessa as he spoke.

Dek rolled her eyes.

"Okay, okay, spare us the morality lessons," Dek said scornfully. "We don't need to hear what you were testing me and Tessa for."

Actually, Tessa wouldn't have minded finding that out. But—well, maybe she already knew.

Dek was still talking.

"Why does it matter what we do?" she asked the computer. "Why do you even need us? If you thought it was best to admit that the whole war was fake, why didn't you and the Westam central computer just tell everyone years ago? Why didn't you pile a bunch of officials onto an airplane and send *them* into the war zone to see it all for themselves?"

"Because all my projections showed that wouldn't work," the voice said, almost a whisper now. "Anything I did on my own—or even with the Westam computer—all of that would be seen as a malfunction. I would have been shut down instantly, before I had a chance to explain. You kids—you're more believable."

Gideon frowned, even as he smoothed down his hair. On their way to the control room he'd detoured past a closet with spare uniforms, so he was back in sparkling, pristine white and gold.

But he still had dirt and blood caked in his hair, and if anything the bruises on his face had gotten darker.

He looked like a hero who hadn't had time to recover from his wounds.

"General Kantoff didn't believe us," Gideon growled. "You could tell—he didn't even think for a moment about the possibility that we might be telling the truth."

"The generals are going to be the hardest ones to convince," the computer voice said patiently. "You think you've spent *your* whole life on the war? They have too—and that's been forty, fifty, sixty years of believing lies are true."

"That's why we have to tell everyone all at once," Tessa said. "The entire country. And Westam, too."

This was the plan they'd come up with: a broadcast to the entire continent. Tessa found that she remembered enough about TV and radio waves to imagine their news floating out everywhere, into the dark corners of Waterford City, across the empty stretches of the war zone, into the foreign cities of the enemy.

And what would happen then? Would people cheer and dance in the streets?

Or would they be angry? Would they feel cheated, learning that everything they'd devoted their lives to for more than seventy-five years was all a scam?

"What if this starts a real war?" Dek asked nervously. "What if Westam starts sending real bombers over here, and we start sending real bombers over there? I mean, if there's not enough water for everyone—"

"There was always enough water," the voice said

scornfully. "People just didn't want to share." The computer made a sound like a sigh. "The Westam system and I won't let anyone start a real fight immediately after your announcement. We'll have everything locked down. All the weapons, all the bombs. But eventually it will be possible to override our controls. . . . You'll have to be very convincing. You'll have to make it so that the majority of the people in each country want peace."

Is that possible? Tessa wondered.

She remembered the little boys back on the dirt pile behind her apartment building, the way they already wanted to fight even at five or six or seven years old.

The way she herself had wanted to beat them up. Had tried to, even.

What if humans are just going to be at war, no matter what? What if it's better if we can all just believe the war is going on, and nobody gets killed for real?

But Dek's parents had been killed by the fake war. Tessa's parents had had their dreams and hopes dashed by a society that poured everything into the war, and nothing into even replacing lightbulbs.

And what about Gideon? Tessa thought. *He's been told his whole life that it's right to kill, that he had to—and yet, somehow, something deep inside him objected to that. . . .*

Tessa was thinking so hard that she missed hearing what the others were talking about.

"I agree," Dek was saying now, nodding at Gideon.

"What?" Tessa asked, looking around, bewildered. "What are you agreeing on?"

"We've got the whole broadcast system ready to go," Gideon said, stepping back from something that Tessa guessed was an improvised camera. "We just agreed that you should be the first person to talk."

"*Me?*" Tessa said, so surprised that her voice squeaked.

"You," Gideon said. "Because you're the one who got us here."

Oh, no, Tessa wanted to say. *I didn't put the miniature laptop back together. I didn't program any computers. I didn't fly the airplane. I can't even walk around my own city without getting lost.*

But Gideon stopped her before she could object.

"You're the one who had the will to get here," he said. "The one who always held on to hope."

I didn't always have hope, Tessa wanted to say. *I just always wanted to have hope. And I'm stupid. I'm not good at anything. I'm just a gnat. A flea. A slug.*

But she wasn't. She was a human—for better or for worse.

Gideon was already pointing the camera in her direction.

Tessa took a deep breath. She gave a fleeting thought to wondering why *she* hadn't bothered combing her hair, as Gideon had. And then she decided it didn't matter.

"Several weeks ago I went to an awards ceremony for a hero," Tessa began. "I thought he was a hero because he'd fought in the war. It turned out that that wasn't exactly true. It was true, though, that he was a hero."

Through the haze of lights directed at her, Tessa saw Gideon jerk back in surprise. She smiled at him—and smiled at everyone in her country, everyone in the enemy's country.

"He was a hero," Tessa continued, "because he wanted to

find out the truth. He was a hero because, when he thought he'd done something awful, he wanted to do everything in his power to make it right."

She paused, gathering her thoughts.

"We all have a chance to be heroes now," she said. "We all have to be brave, and face the truth."

It didn't bother her as much as she would have thought, to have the lights and the eye of the camera pointed directly at her. She knew she was talking to some people who would stay cruel, no matter what, and to some people who, given half a chance, would discover reserves of courage and kindness. She just didn't know which side would win, which portion of human nature would outweigh the other.

But she had enough hope to keep talking.

"Won't you join me and Gideon Thrall and Dekaterina Pratel in being heroes?" she asked. "Not heroes in the war—heroes in the peace?"

She imagined the gasps her words would cause, and how the gasps would grow when she and Gideon and Dek explained that everyone on the continent had been living a lie for more than half a century. The way she saw it, the news would be like sunlight bursting into every dark corner of Eastam, of Westam.

She could hear people tugging on the door behind her, someone yelling, "You've got to let us in! You can't do this! Stop!"

She ignored them. She told her story, start to finish, everything she'd seen and heard and witnessed and thought. Then Dek and Gideon talked, throwing in technical details that meant nothing to her. They explained how the computers had fooled everyone, and why that had been necessary.

"But it's not necessary anymore," Gideon said. "We have another chance. We can make a new start. Please—can't we work together?"

Tessa realized that the shouting outside the door had stopped. Did that mean people were listening? Did that mean they believed?

Dek and Gideon finished up and shut down the camera. Outside, everything was still.

"We've got to find out how people are reacting," Tessa whispered. "Can't the computer show us?"

The three of them clustered around the miniature laptop, which Gideon hooked into the master computer.

And there on the screen Tessa could see the auditorium back in Waterford City. People had evidently gathered there when the announcement began. Now they were crammed in together, everyone staring toward the front. Their eyes were wide; their mouths hung agape. Nobody was saying a word.

"They're in shock," Dek said. "They don't know how to react."

Gideon flicked a switch, and the scene changed. A crowd stood by a fence topped with razor wire. Timidly at first, then with greater boldness, the crowd began shoving at the fence. Someone revved up a chainsaw and carved a hole. A teenage boy darted through the hole.

The camera zoomed in on his face as he landed in the dirt on the other side. He looked horrified at what he'd just done, like he just might die from fright.

But he didn't die. He hit the ground and lay there numbly for a moment. Then, slowly, he stood on wobbly legs. A grin spread across his face. He began waving his arms at everyone still on the other side of the fence, clearly saying, *You climb through too! Come on! It's safe!*

"People are crossing the border," Gideon whispered. "They're going into the war zone."

"They actually believe us?" Tessa asked.

"It looks like those people do," Gideon murmured. "But . . ." He flipped another switch.

Now Tessa saw a huge room, so large it was impossible to see from one end to the other.

Hundreds, maybe even thousands, of young people sat at desks in orderly rows advancing across the room. They all sat the same way: crouched over computers, their hands flying across the controls.

"The pilots," Gideon said. "They're still fighting the war. They haven't changed at all."

"No." The computer voice spoke for the first time since Tessa and Gideon and Dek had made their announcement. "They just *look* like they're still fighting. Zoom in on—oh, try row 600, desk 52."

Gideon adjusted the view, and the camera zoomed in on a screen toward the back of the room.

The screen was filled, not with a battle scene, but with six words: *We have to check this out.*

"He just got that message from his buddy in row 989, desk 40," the computer voice said. "Fifty percent of the pilots have their computers set on Automatic and are trying to verify what the three of you just said. No, it's seventy-five percent now. Eighty percent. Ninety. And—oh, wow—that was fast!"

"What?" Tessa asked.

"Five pilots are trying to make contact with someone in the Westam military," the voice said. "No, eight. Twenty. Forty . . ."

Gideon dropped the miniature laptop. His eyes bugged out, but he seemed too stunned even to bend over and pick it up again.

"The war is over," he said. "This is the end of everything."

Tessa reached out and gently took his hand in hers.

"No," she corrected. "It's the beginning."

ABOUT THE AUTHOR

MARGARET PETERSON HADDIX is the author of many critically and popularly acclaimed books for children and teens, including *Claim to Fame*, *Palace of Mirrors*, *Uprising*, The Missing series, and the Shadow Children series. A graduate of Miami University (of Ohio), Margaret Peterson Haddix worked for several years as a reporter for the *Indianapolis News*. She also taught at the Danville (Illinois) Area Community College. She lives with her husband and two children in Columbus, Ohio.